MURDER IN VENICE

T. A. WILLIAMS

B

Boldwood

First published in Great Britain in 2025 by Boldwood Books Ltd.

Copyright © T. A. Williams, 2025

Cover Design by JD Smith Design Ltd

Cover Images: Shutterstock

The moral right of T. A. Williams to be identified as the author of this work has been asserted in accordance with the Copyright, Designs and Patents Act 1988.

A CIP catalogue record for this book is available from the British Library.

Paperback ISBN 978-1-83703-127-6

Large Print ISBN 978-1-83703-128-3

Hardback ISBN 978-1-83703-126-9

Trade Paperback ISBN 978-1-80656-046-2

Ebook ISBN 978-1-83703-129-0

Kindle ISBN 978-1-83703-130-6

Audio CD ISBN 978-1-83703-121-4

MP3 CD ISBN 978-1-83703-122-1

Digital audio download ISBN 978-1-83703-123-8

This book is printed on certified sustainable paper. Boldwood Books is dedicated to putting sustainability at the heart of our business. For more information please visit https://www.boldwoodbooks.com/about-us/sustainability/

Boldwood Books Ltd, 23 Bowerdean Street, London, SW6 3TN

www.boldwoodbooks.com

To Mariangela with love as ever – remembering our last trip to Venice together.

1

MONDAY MORNING

That Monday started off pretty much the same as any other Monday – until I received a phone call. It came as I was sitting at a table outside a little café just on the edge of Florence's *centro storico*, enjoying an espresso before heading back to the office. It was only ten o'clock in the morning, but the temperature was already soaring. July in Florence can be very, very hot, and the presence of tens, if not hundreds, of thousands of tourists in the city didn't make things any easier. Oscar was sprawled in the shade at my feet with his tongue out. Although he was born here, it can't be a bundle of fun walking around in a black fur coat all the time. It had been a potentially stressful last half-hour, and I had brought him along in the hope that his presence might be of some comfort to Signora Benedetti – but as it had turned out, his presence, while welcome, hadn't been necessary.

In my relatively new career as a private investigator, it hadn't taken me long to realise that a considerable amount of my time was going to be occupied with cases involving marital infidelity. Whether this is a reflection on the dubious quality of television here in Italy, or whether there's some deep-rooted Latin lover instinct buried inside so many Italian men, it had rapidly become clear to me that a considerable proportion of the Italian male population view fidelity as a challenge rather than an obligation. This morning, I had had to break the news to a client named Signora Benedetti that her suspicions about her husband had been fully justified and I had handed her over a collection of incriminating photos of him with his paramour to prove it. Interestingly, her reaction had not been what might have been expected. Instead of anger or grief, I had distinctly sensed satisfaction, and it hadn't taken me long to work out that she was only too pleased to have been handed the proof she needed to divorce him and make a fresh start.

It was as I sat and sipped my scalding-hot coffee that the call came through. To my considerable surprise, I saw that it was from Selena. Selena Gardner was one of the most famous and recognisable faces – and bodies – in the world. She was an acting superstar who had appeared in countless movies and could rightly be considered as at the pinnacle of her profession, a true Hollywood icon. I had met her almost two years earlier when she had been in Florence making a movie, and I had helped the local police track down a delusional killer intent on stopping production of the film by any means, including murder. I hadn't heard from her since then and I hadn't expected to. She inhabited a very different world from my own, so my curiosity was immediately aroused by the call.

'Hi, Selena, long time no speak.'

'Dan, darling, how wonderful to speak to you.' Her voice was like warm caramel, and in spite of my being in a very happy relationship with my fiancée, Anna, I still felt a thrill. Of course, I reminded myself, she was an actor, and turning on the charm was second nature to her. Still, I had to admit that she did sound genuinely pleased to speak to me. 'First things first, have you married Anna yet?'

I couldn't help smiling. Two years ago, it had been her match-making that had thrown Anna and me together. 'Not yet, but I've asked her to marry me, and she's said yes.'

I heard her give a happy chortle. 'I knew it! I said you were perfect for each other, didn't I?' She didn't give me a chance to reply. 'Do give her my love, won't you?'

I promised her that I would, and we exchanged a few more pleasantries. She told me she was in Paris to pick up an award – she sounded less than thrilled at the prospect of yet another accolade – but that it was a flying visit, and she wouldn't have time to come to Tuscany. She promised that she would come sooner or later, and I said she was always welcome, all the while wondering what had made this cinema legend decide to contact a mere mortal like me. It wasn't long before she satisfied my curiosity.

'Dan, darling, you've heard of Alice Graceland, haven't you?'

I certainly had. '*The* Alice Graceland?' Alice Graceland was another superstar of the cinema, British rather than American, probably around my age. Over the past four decades, she had been every bit as much of a celebrity as Selena was now, starting as a stunningly beautiful starlet playing opposite cinema legends and household names. Over the past ten years, she had become known to television viewers the world over for her role as Elisa Banbury, supersleuth, a modern-day, younger and sexier Miss Marple, with a plethora of movies and TV series to her name. I, like so many of my contemporaries, had enjoyed watching the beautiful English-woman as she solved apparently insoluble crimes from London to Los Angeles. What, I wondered, had such a celebrity to do with me?

Selena didn't leave me in suspense for long. 'Yes, I've known

Alice for years now. I've acted alongside her a few times, and we live not far from each other in Beverly Hills. Anyway, we were talking, and she wants you to call her.'

'She wants to talk to *me*? She knows who I am?'

'She does now.'

'Wow!'

My mind was racing. Why me? Could it be my books? All my life, I'd dreamt of becoming a published author and now, since giving up my job as a detective chief inspector at Scotland Yard three years earlier, I had finally found the time to write a couple of whodunnits and, to my amazement, had had the great good fortune to find a publisher prepared to publish them. The books were selling pretty well, but I hadn't realised that my fame might now have extended to Hollywood. 'Did she say why she wants me to call her?' Thoughts of a possible movie contract flashed through my head. Might this mean that my books might end up being turned into films?

Selena's answer wasn't what I was expecting.

'She's having a party, and she wants to invite you.'

'She wants me to come to her party?' I couldn't believe my ears. I felt a movement at my feet and I glanced down to see Oscar staring up at me with a concerned look on his face. I reached down and gave his ears a reassuring scratch as Selena replied.

'It's not just a social call. She asked me to ask you to call her as soon as possible on *a matter of importance*.'

My mind was racing. Importance to whom? To her or to me? I felt a wave of excitement shoot through me as Selena rattled off Alice Graceland's phone number, and I realised as I wrote it down that it was an Italian number. Presumably, this meant she was here in the country. Might I even get to meet this legendary star?

Selena and I chatted a bit more before she blew me a couple of kisses and the call ended, leaving me intrigued to find out why Alice Graceland, *the* Alice Graceland, wanted to talk to me.

I set the phone back on the table and looked down at Oscar. Aware that he was being observed, he started thumping the end of his tail softly against the ground, and I took this as a sign of interest.

'Alice Graceland, Oscar! Do you know what this might mean?'

No doubt stirred by the enthusiasm in my voice, he pulled himself to his feet and looked up at me with his head resting against my knee.

'Alice Graceland is a big, huge star, just about as big as it gets, cinema and TV royalty, maybe even bigger than Selena. If she wants to see me, might this mean she's read my books? Could this be the start of something amazing?'

The end of his tail wagged another couple of times before he decided that he would leave me to make the phone call by myself. He settled back down again with a sigh, and I saw his eyes close as he relaxed once more. As I looked down at him, I reflected that I would do well to follow his example. There was no point in getting too excited at this stage. Alice Graceland was most likely interested in employing me in my role as a private investigator, no doubt on the recommendation of Selena. She probably didn't even know I'd written the books. Alternatively, maybe she was simply on the lookout for some information about police procedure from a real-life ex-copper to help her acting career. I made a conscious effort to dampen my enthusiasm before picking the phone up again. I swallowed the last of my coffee, almost scalding my tongue in the process, but feeling that I needed the caffeine boost, before punching in the number and pressing the green button.

My call was answered almost immediately by the voice of a woman who hedged her bets by giving me a bilingual greeting.

'*Pronto*, hello.'

This didn't sound like the Alice Graceland I remembered from the movies, so I assumed it to be a secretary. Presumably the grande dame didn't answer her own phone.

I spoke in English. 'Hello, my name's Armstrong, Dan Armstrong. I've been asked to speak to Alice Graceland. Is now a good time?'

There was recognition in her voice when she answered. 'Of course, Mr Armstrong, I'll put you through.' The line went dead for only a couple of seconds before I heard a different and instantly recognisable voice.

'Mr Armstrong, hello. I'm delighted to hear from you. Thank you for calling.' Hearing her voice took me back to old times sitting on the sofa with my ex-wife, wishing I could solve crimes with the panache of Alice Graceland. Her English accent on the phone to me was far less pronounced than the posh accent she adopted in her Elisa Banbury mysteries.

I took a deep breath and responded. 'Good morning, I'm only too happy to speak to you.'

'Can I ask where you're calling from?'

'I'm in Florence. I live and work here now.'

'If you're not too busy, I'd be very grateful if you could come and see me as soon as you can. Might that be possible? If so, when do you think you could you get here?'

'Where are you calling from? Are you in Florence as well?'

'I'm sorry, I should have said. I'm in Venice. Would you be able to come up and see me here?'

I thought quickly. Venice is almost three hundred kilometres north of Florence. In spite of having lived in Italy now for three years, I had yet to visit that famous city, although it was high on my bucket list. As far as I could remember, I didn't have anything too pressing on my agenda this week. 'I could probably come as soon as tomorrow or Wednesday. I'll have to check with the office to see what appointments I've got. I can call you back in a couple of minutes.'

'That sounds excellent, thank you. I do hope you'll be able to make it. I look forward to hearing from you.' She sounded pleased, and when the call ended, I glanced down at Oscar.

'What do you reckon? Is this my entry to the wonderful world of Hollywood, or is it something more banal?'

Oscar's ear twitched, but he didn't bother to open his eyes, so I called Lina at the office. She is my PA, receptionist, telephonist, occasional dog walker and friend, as well as being the wife of Virgilio, my best friend here in Italy. Commissario Virgilio Pisano is a senior police officer in the Florence murder squad, and we have a lot in common. He sometimes asks me to work alongside him, particularly when the case involves English speakers. Employing Lina has made my life a whole lot easier – not least because she handles the endless stream of Italian bureaucracy and, more importantly today, my diary.

I told her I had to go to Venice, and she confirmed that she felt sure she could rearrange the only appointment I had scheduled for tomorrow so that I could head north. I asked her to do that and told her I would explain what it was all about when I got back to the office. I immediately phoned Alice Graceland back. This time, she answered the call herself.

'Mr Armstrong? Thanks for calling back. Are you going to be able to come and see me?'

'Yes, indeed, I can come tomorrow.'

'That's excellent.' She sounded delighted, and my spirits rose some more. 'Give me your email and I'll get my PA to send you a train ticket.'

I was tempted to tell her that I might consider driving but, in fairness, this would involve three hours on the road each way, so maybe the train was the sensible option. I dictated my email and was about to ask her for her address in Venice when she surprised me.

'I'll send my PA to collect you from the station.'

'How will I recognise him or her?'

I heard an amused note in her voice. 'You're the private investigator, DCI Armstrong; you'll work it out.'

I set down my phone on the table with mixed feelings. On the one hand, I was intrigued and excited at the prospect of meeting such a big-name actor and, in spite of my best efforts to temper my expectations, I couldn't help wondering whether this might presage some major step forward in my literary career. However, I told myself firmly that she almost certainly wanted me in my capacity as a private investigator.

I called Anna to give her the news, and she sounded fascinated. When discussing our forthcoming wedding over the past weeks since I had popped the question, and she had said yes, she and I had even toyed with the idea of slipping away for a quiet wedding in, of all places, Venice, but that was still in the melting pot. Considering that she had been born and bred in Florence and was immensely proud of her home town, I had been surprised to hear her describe Venice to me as the most amazing city in the world.

In view of her love of the city, I asked her if she wanted to come with me the following day. I suggested that she could take Oscar for a walk around the 'amazing city' and look for possible wedding venues while I had my meeting with the famous actor, but she had no hesitation in refusing.

'Venice in the middle of July? You must be joking! If you think Florence is crowded at the moment, you can double or treble that for Venice. Here at least there are lots of streets for the tourists to wander around, but in Venice, the main roads are canals and many of the streets are little more than narrow walkways. Poor Oscar would probably be trampled underfoot and I wouldn't do much better. No, you go and see your Hollywood icon, and I'll stay here and look after Oscar, but don't say I didn't warn you about the crowds.'

Oscar and I exchanged glances. I would be sorry not to have him with me – he's pretty much a permanent fixture at my side these days – but I knew Anna was right. Besides, she would spoil him rotten in my absence, and that would suit him down to the ground.

2

TUESDAY MORNING

Next morning, I caught the 9.20 *Frecciarossa* high-speed train to Venice. I was impressed to find that Alice Graceland's PA had booked me tickets in business class rather than normal second class, and I had to admit that the journey was a lot more comfortable and relaxing than it would have been in my Volkswagen minivan.

I spent some of the journey checking out Alice Graceland on the Internet. I had imagined her to be a year or two older than me and I was almost right. She was in fact four years older, making her sixty-two, almost sixty-three. She had been born in the sixties and her breakthrough into the movie business had come when she was discovered in a talent show in Blackpool at the age of just sixteen. From then on, the trajectory of her career had been ballistic, and her Wikipedia page listed a dazzling array of awards she had won, from Emmys to Oscars.

There were numerous photos of her, and I could trace her right back to her early roles as a clueless, if gorgeous, teenager in saucy UK comedies to more serious and, inevitably, more challenging roles in the following years after she had made the transition to Hollywood and international stardom. She had married in her forties and this had lasted for ten years or so but had come to a premature end eleven years ago when her husband had suddenly died of heart failure. Many of the photos showed her in the company of the biggest Hollywood personalities, and I found my hopes for my career soaring once again. Could it be that she was about to introduce me into that high-octane world? Was this the start of something big? I did my best to temper my expectations, but I was in a state of considerable anticipation by the time I got to Venice.

The train arrived bang on time, and the last couple of kilometres were remarkable for the fact that the railway line ran along a narrow causeway leading to the city, through the grey-green water of the Venetian lagoon that stretched out on both sides. The station, Venezia Santa Lucia, is at the end of the line, and when the train stopped, I saw all the passengers streaming along the platform towards the exit beyond the front of the train.

As for working out how I would recognise Alice Graceland's PA, who was supposed to be meeting me, in fact, it hadn't been difficult – it would be up to *them* to recognise *me*. My carriage and seat number had been clearly marked on the E-ticket she had emailed to me. In consequence, it came as no surprise to find a young woman waiting on the platform for me when I climbed down from the train. Presumably, she had been given my description or shown my photo and had been primed. She stepped forward and held out her hand.

'Mr Armstrong, welcome to Venice.' I recognised her voice as that of the person who had fielded my first call to Alice Graceland the previous day.

She looked as if she was in her mid-twenties and she had a friendly smile on her face. I felt sure that Oscar would have given her his seal of approval; he likes the ladies. We shook hands and she introduced herself.

'My name's Mary Stevenson. I'm Miss Graceland's PA. I hope you've had a comfortable trip.' Her accent was educated southern English, maybe Home Counties. I assured her that the trip had been excellent, and we joined the stream of people all heading towards the exit. As we walked, I asked her how long she had been working for Alice Graceland, and it turned out that she was very new to the post.

'I started exactly one month ago. I love Venice, but I must say, I hadn't expected it to be quite so hot.'

In true English tradition, we talked about the weather, and I told her that Florence was equally oppressive at this time of year. We made our way out through a collection of shops at the end of the platform until we emerged through the glass doors of the crowded entrance hall into the full force of the sun, blazing down from a cloudless sky. I reached for my sunglasses and had to agree with her that Venice was every bit as hot as Florence, maybe even more so today. Like many of the people emerging from the station, I found myself pausing on the brick-paved piazza to take in my surroundings. It felt somehow surreal to be only a few steps from the hi-tech twenty-first-century technology behind us and yet to be instantly immersed in a scene that probably hadn't changed very much in the last five hundred years. Directly in front of us, the paved area ended at the edge of a broad canal with, bizarrely, what looked like a refuse truck transplanted into a barge chugging past between no fewer than three green and white passenger ferries.

Mary glanced across at me. 'Seeing as you live in Italy, I suppose you've been here lots of times before.'

I shook my head. 'It's on my must-see list, but this is the first time I've been here. You'll have to forgive me if I take a moment or two to get my head around what I'm looking at.'

She smiled again. 'Like I say, I've been here for a month, but I still find it the most amazing place. Just think boats instead of cars, canals in place of roads, ferries instead of buses. It takes a bit of getting used to.'

And it did. Doing my best to ignore the crowds of people milling around – almost all of them tourists, as far as I could see – I let my eyes roam over the scene that had opened up in front of me. The canal was wider than I had expected, easily as wide as a four-lane highway, and it was lined with predominantly pink-, cream- and ochre-coloured buildings, not one of them identical to its neighbour. Directly in front of me was an impressive old church capped with a bulbous dome, and with massive stone pillars at the front. As my eyes gradually became more accustomed to the scene, I realised that, as well as the bigger vessels, the canal was full of smaller boats of all sizes and even a pair of shiny, black gondolas, expertly sculled by gondoliers in their trademark striped tops and straw boaters.

'Diego is just down there.' Mary's voice interrupted my observations.

I followed the direction of her pointing finger with my eyes and saw an impeccable shiny wooden launch waiting at the bottom of the steps leading down to the water's edge, bobbing gently up and down as the wakes of the bigger vessels sent little waves across the water. It looked as though we were going to be travelling in style. Mary led the way and we both stepped aboard while Diego expertly kept the boat in position alongside the quay. As soon as we were both on board, I heard the engine pick up, and he headed out to join the flotilla of other vessels on the canal. Although there was a cabin with red velvet cushions on the seats, Mary and I both opted to stand outside in the open at the stern and admire the view. Mary helpfully gave me a running commentary as we chugged down the canal, under bridges and past sumptuous buildings, each one more intricate and amazing than the next.

'This is the Grand Canal. As you probably know, Venice is made up of a number of islands, and the Grand Canal bisects the main part of the city. We're heading south now, and our journey takes us past some of the most famous sights in the world.'

Still somewhat dazed by the overwhelming sense of history that Venice had inspired in me, I reluctantly dragged my mind back to the present. 'Where exactly are we going?'

'We're on our way to Miss Graceland's home – at least one of her homes. She also has a house in California and a flat in London – I haven't been to either yet – but she tells me she's planning to spend much of her time here nowadays. There's a strict speed limit all over the lagoon, so it'll take us about twenty minutes to get to the Swan's Nest.'

'That's the name of her house?' I gave her a grin. 'That doesn't sound very Italian.'

Her face crinkled into a smile. 'That's what she calls the place where she lives. Miss Graceland hardly speaks any Italian, so it's easier for her in English. Her home is quite something, so I won't spoil the surprise by telling you anything more about it for now.'

'That sounds intriguing. I look forward to seeing it. And what about your Italian? Do you speak it?'

'I'm pretty fluent.' Just in case I might have any doubts on this score, she continued in far better Italian than mine. 'My mum was Italian and, although I was born and brought up in the UK, she always spoke to me in Italian, so I couldn't help learning it.'

I nodded approvingly. '*Complimenti*. By the way, I note that you refer to your employer as "Miss Graceland". Is that what she prefers to be called?'

She reverted to English. 'Yes, she prefers "Miss Graceland". I imagine she'll want you to address her in the same way.'

After this, she continued to reel off the names of the principal sights as we made our way down the canal. The waterway was wider down here, certainly every bit as wide as a six-lane *autostrada* – and it needed to be. I lost count of the number of boats of all shapes and sizes that we passed on the way, and I realised that Mary was right. What we were travelling along was in fact Venice's main street that just happened to be made of water rather than tarmac. As well as ferries, gondolas, launches and other boats carrying passengers, there were more utilitarian vessels piled high with goods destined for the city's shops, police launches decked out in the same blue and white colours as normal squad cars, and an ambulance boat equipped with a flashing blue light. Instead of having drives or garages, the houses lining the canal had hefty posts the thickness of telegraph poles planted in front of them where boats could moor up alongside wooden jetties leading into the properties. The tops of the posts were painted in a range of different colours – no doubt to help the postman when he did his rounds in yet another boat – and I did my best to come to terms with this unique aquatic environment.

As we passed under the Rialto Bridge, I could see from the mass of figures up there that it was absolutely packed with humanity, as were all the narrow lanes and streets that appeared from time to time between the magnificent *palazzi*. I spared a thought for Oscar. It looked to me as if Venice was no place for a dog. We had been travelling for ten minutes already, and I still hadn't spotted a single green open space. Yes, Oscar would have loved the water – although I did wonder how clean it could be with so many buildings and people surrounding it – but I had the feeling I would struggle to find him somewhere to run around if he were to accompany me next time I came here. For humans, on the other hand, as long as they didn't mind crowds, it was a stunning place. Mary continued to produce place names for me until we reached what looked like an intricate wooden bridge spanning the canal.

'That's the Galleria dell'Accademia over there to the right.' She pointed ahead, through the arch of the bridge. 'I visited the gallery last week and it's packed with masterpieces by some of the most famous Venetian artists of all time like Titian and Canaletto.'

I filed that information away to pass on to Anna – although she probably knew this already – and decided to bring the conversation back to Mary's employer. 'Does Miss Graceland give you some decent time off?'

She nodded. 'I certainly can't complain about my working hours.'

The way she said it, I got the feeling she might have complaints about other aspects of her job. I didn't spend thirty years as a detective for nothing, so I gave her a gentle push. 'What's it like working for such a cinema legend?'

A shadow flitted across her face for a fraction of a second before she replied with an air of assumed positivity. 'It's an amazing opportunity for me. I've just finished a doctorate in media studies – my thesis was on powerful female figures of TV and cinema. As you can imagine, Miss Graceland is one of the most significant. Like I say, it's a terrific opportunity.' Her voice tailed off a bit at the end, and I couldn't help giving her another prompt.

'A terrific opportunity but...? Is the job maybe not quite what you were expecting? Is Miss Graceland not what you were expecting?'

Her cheeks flushed, and for a moment, I thought she was

going to give me an honest answer, but then she just produced a little smile. 'I'm not sure what I was expecting, really. But she's been very kind to me, and it's a real privilege being able to work with an actor of her stature.'

I didn't blame her for her reticence. She didn't know me from Adam, and if she had opened up to me about any doubts, she had no way of knowing whether I would go running to her employer to pass on the information. I smiled back and transferred my attention to a gondola that emerged from a very narrow side canal and glided sedately directly across the Grand Canal, somehow managing to avoid being bulldozed out of the way by the succession of far bigger vessels travelling up and down. I filed Mary's hesitation away for future reference. It sounded as though Alice Graceland maybe wasn't the easiest of employers, but I had heard enough about spoiled Hollywood stars not to be surprised by this. At that moment, we emerged from the Grand Canal into a much wider waterway, and Mary was quick to change back to tourist guide again.

'On the right are the islands of San Giorgio Maggiore and Giudecca, and up ahead on the left, you can see the famous belltower, and in a few moments, we'll be able to see into St Mark's square. Check out the Palazzo Ducale and St Mark's Basilica, the cathedral. It's one of the most iconic views in the world. Every time I come past here, I imagine how life must have been for the Doge, the overall ruler of the Republic, back in medieval and Renaissance times.'

I stood and gazed in silent awe at the view. All along the quayside to our left, there were glossy, black gondolas moored against wooden posts, while behind them was a symphony of white stone buildings with countless columns, arches, statues, domes and spires. Towering above everything was the red brick and white marble campanile with a golden archangel Gabriel at the very top, but with the winged lion, the symbol of Venice, proudly displayed at the top of the façade not far below the angel. I had seen it numerous times in photos and on TV but seeing it at first-hand was stunning. Equally stunning was the mass of people filling the square. There must have been thousands of tourists milling around there, and I spared a thought for ordinary Venetians trying to go about their daily work. Certainly, being a postman trying to do his rounds here was likely to take considerable patience.

The water became slightly rougher as we left the Grand Canal behind us and emerged into the open waters of the lagoon. Ahead of us was a long spit of land covered in buildings that Mary told me was the Lido – effectively the barrier separating Venice from the Adriatic sea beyond. At first, it looked as though we were going to be heading there, but I was in for a surprise. As we approached a small island to our right, more like a fortress built of red bricks with walls the height of a two- or three-storey house, Diego, our driver – or should that be our captain? – slowed the engine, spun the wheel and turned towards it. He drew up alongside a stone jetty below what looked like the only entrance to the fortress – an arched doorway set in the massive walls – and he expertly moored up behind a smaller wooden boat with its outboard motor tilted up out of the water. Mary shot me a triumphant glance.

'I said it would be a surprise, didn't I? This is one of a number of fortifications built to defend the city. This one dates back to the fourteenth century and its Italian name is the *Isola dei Cigni*, literally the Island of the Swans. Miss Graceland bought it two years ago and the builders only finished the total renovation and restructuring of the place last winter. You wait – it's amazing inside.' She sounded understandably impressed.

She was right to be impressed. I certainly hadn't been

expecting a private island, and for a moment, I found myself thinking of numerous James Bond movies involving evil villains intent on world domination living on private islands. Hopefully, I wouldn't find Miss Graceland stroking a Persian cat and threatening to feed me to her pet sharks, piranhas or alligators.

I gave Mary a smile. 'I've come across some amazing villas and castles in Tuscany, but nothing to compete with this. Fancy having your own island...'

I followed her out onto the jetty, and she led me to the arched entrance.

'Welcome to the Swan's Nest, Mr Armstrong.'

3

The hefty wooden door – about a foot thick and studded with nails whose heads were the size of golf balls – was open, and a stone ramp led up to the daylight beyond. As we climbed the steep slope, I did a quick calculation and reckoned that the walls were probably as much as four or five metres thick and the same kind of height – definitely built to repel even the most deter-mined assault. When we emerged at the top of the ramp, it was to find ourselves in a totally unexpected environment. Secluded by the surrounding walls was an enchanting sub-tropical garden half the size of a football pitch, with palm trees, exotic shrubs and, at the centre, a swimming pool surrounded by lavender and rosemary bushes. All around were buildings constructed against the inside of the defensive walls which, presumably, had once housed the garrison.

I followed Mary along a paved path through the bushes to the largest of the buildings. A series of arches along the front had been glazed and they looked out onto a charming terrace protected from the sun by a wrought-iron pergola covered in luxuriant vines. She led me along the terrace until she reached a glass door. She tapped on it and, without waiting for an answer, held it open for me.

'This is Miss Graceland's study. She'll see you here. *Arrivederci*, Signor Armstrong.' She spoke in hushed tones as she ushered me inside before closing the door quietly behind me and leaving me on my own.

I stood still and took stock. It was a large room for a study, and although there was a bookcase full of books, including one whole shelf of gardening books – presumably the film star's hobby – the focal point of the room was a massive TV screen mounted on the end wall. Compared to the outside temperature, it was blissfully cool in here and I could see that a new air-conditioning system had been installed. Directly in front of me was a big, old-fashioned wooden desk with a modern office chair behind it, but there was no sign of my host. The desktop was piled high with untidy heaps of paper, most covered in scribbled handwriting, and there was a large-screen laptop closed in the centre of it. There was a fine old wooden door set in the wall to my left, presumably connecting with the rest of the house, and a pair of stylish, modern sofas to the right, facing each other across a glass-topped coffee table. The vaulted brick ceiling had quite clearly been recently sandblasted, and the room had been replastered and repainted. The floor was paved with light-grey marble slabs – probably not original – strewn with handsome Persian rugs, and the overall impression was of comfort and understated opulence.

I heard footsteps approaching, and the door on my left opened. I turned at the sound of the door handle and found myself in the presence of a true megastar. I recognised Alice Graceland immediately, and my first impression was that she surely couldn't be over sixty. She was casually dressed in a blue skirt and a T-shirt advertising The Eagles' comeback tour at

Madison Square Garden, and she looked stunning. As her bright-blue eyes – either by accident or design, the exact same shade as her skirt – met mine, she produced a radiant smile that threatened to reduce me to a gibbering wreck, fiancée or no fiancée. She was a stunningly attractive woman, and I found myself smiling gormlessly back at her. She walked over to where I was standing and extended an elegant hand.

'Mr Armstrong, good morning. Thank you for coming.'

Close up, I could see a handful of fine lines around her eyes, but she could very easily have passed for ten or even twenty years younger than me. Mind you, a lot of people look younger than me these days.

'I'm very pleased to meet you, Miss Graceland. It's an honour to meet an actor of your stature.'

She gave me a deprecating smile. 'You're too kind. Please take a seat. I'd like to talk to you.'

I sat down on one of the leather sofas facing her and she took a seat opposite me.

'The reason I've invited you here is because, at the end of the month, I'm having a house party, and I would like you to come.' No doubt noticing my puzzled expression, which had been there since Selena had told me about the invitation, she elaborated. 'I want you here in your professional capacity. I'm going to need you for your expertise as a detective, and I insist on paying you for your time.'

Conflicting thoughts were going through my head. There was a certain amount of disappointment, although even in my most optimistic moments, I hadn't really been expecting her to offer to turn my books into blockbuster movies. This sense of disappointment was tempered by the thought of who might be at this party. Was I likely to find myself surrounded by famous faces and maybe even Hollywood film producers interested in turning my books into movies? Along with this was natural curiosity to know exactly why she felt she needed the presence of a private investigator at the party. Before I could ask, she explained.

'It's going to be a murder mystery weekend.' I probably looked a bit vague, so she gave me more detail. 'I don't know if you've ever been to one before, but the idea is that, with the aid of a few actors, I give my guests a good dinner and in the course of it, I present them with a murder – naturally, a fictitious murder – and they have to sniff out the culprit or culprits.'

I gave her a smile in return. 'That sounds interesting, but a murder mystery weekend is a new one on me. I must admit that, during my thirty years at Scotland Yard, I tended to get more than my fair share of real murder investigations without going out and looking for more. It's very kind of you to think of me and, to be quite honest, seeing as most of my life now as a PI tends to consist mainly of marital infidelity and petty crime, it'll be good to get involved with a murder investigation where nobody gets killed. Where's the party going to take place – here?'

She nodded. 'It'll be the first opportunity I've had to show the place off. The builders only finished just before Christmas.'

'Will your guests be staying here, or will they be staying in hotels?'

'There will only be a dozen or so people, so they can all stay here, yourself included. There are twelve guest bedrooms, so there's ample space. By the way, I gather from Selena that you and your dog are a double act. Do bring it with you, by all means. I love dogs and I'll write it into the murder mystery script.'

'That's very kind. I'll tell him to be on his best behaviour. When exactly is the party taking place? You mentioned the end of the month.'

'The invitations have gone out for people to come a week on Saturday. Most people will arrive in the morning, so we'll lay on lunch here, and the main event will be a big dinner that night, and that will include the murder mystery. Sunday will be more informal, with the opportunity for those who're interested to do some sightseeing. Sunday will also be the day when I can sit down and talk to some of my guests. I expect people will head off again on Monday.'

'Could I ask who these people are going to be? Will they be family members, friends, business associates, fellow actors? I imagine they're people you know and trust.'

'They're a mix of actors and movie people – you know, producers, directors, that sort of thing.'

I felt my hopes soar again at the thought of rubbing shoulders with what would undoubtedly be a highly influential group of people. Maybe people looking for a couple of murder mysteries to turn into blockbuster movies?

Unaware of my high hopes, she carried on. 'I know what you're going to say: you're going to ask me why I'm inviting *you* in particular. After all, you aren't from the TV or movie world. The answer is that you have what none of the people at the party actually have – me included – and that's direct personal experience of real murder investigations. People know me as Elisa Banbury, supersleuth, but I'm a fraud – I just recite the lines they give me. I want my murder mystery to be as authentic as possible, and what could be more authentic than a real live Scotland Yard detective running things?'

'I can't thank you enough but, given my lack of experience of these murder mystery games, you're going to have to talk me through what you want me to do, if I really am going to be running things.'

'Don't worry, I'll see that you're well briefed, and we'll have a full rehearsal before the event. As for what you'll be doing, it's quite simple really: I'd like you to play the part of an investigator, a detective, not dissimilar to DCI Armstrong of the Metropolitan Police.'

I smiled back. 'I think I should just about be able to remember how to do that.'

'Excellent. Although the guests will be arriving a week on Saturday, would you be able to come on the Friday, so we can do a dummy run of the event with the actors that evening? That way, we should all know what we're doing.' I nodded in agreement and she glanced at her watch. 'Twelve-thirty already. We mustn't keep Valentina waiting.' She jumped to her feet. 'Let's go and have lunch while I tell you more about what awaits you at the end of the month.'

I followed her out through the door onto the terrace and along to the next building. Here, she ushered me into a large dining room with a table in the middle big enough for twenty people. We perched rather forlornly at one end of it.

Lunch was exquisite. The meal had been prepared by Diego's wife, Valentina, and I learned that she, together with her husband, had come to live on the island, where they looked after Miss Graceland's home throughout the year. Alice Graceland told me that she had been exceptionally lucky to find such a talented pair, and I soon realised what she meant. Over an amazingly tasty starter consisting of a salad of fresh crab meat mixed with slices of apple and pieces of a hard blue cheese, she told me that Valentina and her husband did everything from tending the garden to cleaning the house, and that their daughter, who lived in Mestre, just outside Venice on the mainland, was going to come and assist when the house party took place.

After the antipasti, Valentina arrived with homemade *crespelle*. Unknown to her, these folded pancakes stuffed with cheese and ham are some of my all-time favourite Italian dishes, and Valentina's tasted excellent. For somebody used to living in

Tuscany, where most meals are accompanied by Chianti – a red wine – it came as an interesting change to find that we were served white wine from an unlabelled bottle. Miss Graceland told me that this was in fact Prosecco. What was particularly interesting about this version was that, when first poured into our glasses, the wine fizzed like the sort of Prosecco with which I was familiar, but then immediately settled down to an extremely palatable table wine. She told me that Diego sourced the wine locally in *damigiane* – fifty-litre glass containers – and bottled it himself. I told her that I did the exact same thing with my local red, which is excellent, but I couldn't fault this white wine either.

The *crespelle* were followed by another of my favourite dishes – *fritto misto*. This lightly fried mix of prawns, squid, whitebait and octopus was exquisite, and I found myself marvelling at how Alice Graceland managed to stay so slim and fit if she ate and drank like this all the time. Later on, unprompted, she offered me an explanation as Valentina served us panna cotta smothered with blueberries in syrup.

'I don't normally eat anything like as much as this. I'm going to have to go for a good long swim and spend an hour in the gym later on.' A look of what might have been regret appeared on her face. 'And then I'll be back on rabbit food again.'

The conversation carried on, covering everything from murder cases I had investigated to life in Italy, and I told her that this sort of meal was also far more than I normally ate. Valentina arrived and asked if me if I would like a *digestivo*, but I thanked her and asked for just an espresso. At the end of the meal, I asked for more details of the people invited to the house party and Miss Graceland's answer was inconclusive.

'I'll get Mary to email you the list when it's finalised. She sent out the invitations a few weeks ago, and some have already said yes, but I'm still waiting to hear from the others. Desmond, that's

Desmond Norman, doesn't like committing himself to anything in a hurry, but I imagine he'll come.'

I immediately recognised the name. Desmond Norman had for many years been the modern-day equivalent of Cecil B. DeMille, probably the most important and influential film producer in the world. He had to be in his eighties now, but I'd heard that his name still commanded massive respect in movie circles.

I was impressed. It looked as though Alice Graceland was inviting the crème de la crème... and me. I suppressed an apprehensive gulp.

'And the others?'

'Mary will supply you with their details as and when they reply but, like I say, they're a mix of people I've known for many, many years.'

'What about wives and girlfriends?'

'Some, but not many... Mary will be able to tell you more.' She glanced at her watch and stood up. Taking the hint, I hastily rose to my feet as she held out her hand to me again. 'Thank you so much for taking the trouble to come and see me. I'm delighted you're going to be able to help out. I've written the script for the murder mystery myself and I plan on showing some of these big-noise directors and producers, not only that I'm the best actor they've ever worked with, but that I can do their own jobs better than they can, too.' Her eyes sparkled as we shook hands. 'I'm not really that conceited, Mr Armstrong. It's just that Hollywood is still very much a boys' club, and it'll be fun to show them what a woman can do. Now, I think it's time for me to have a little siesta – it always happens when I drink at lunchtime – but Mary will be pleased to show you around before Diego takes you back to catch your train. I look forward to seeing you at the end of next week.'

4

TUESDAY AFTERNOON

Mary was sitting outside on the terrace reading a book. She looked up as I appeared and gave me a bright smile.

'Good lunch?'

'An amazing lunch. If I had a cook like Valentina, I'd be the size of a Zeppelin by now.' I went on to ask her what time I needed to leave to be sure of catching the three-thirty train. She told me that any time before three should be fine – traffic jams in Venice are a rarity – so I asked her if she could drag herself away from her reading material to show me around the island first.

She picked up a dry bougainvillaea leaf from the ground and used it to mark her page in the book. 'Is there anywhere special you'd like to see?'

'The whole place, really. I imagine Miss Graceland has told you that she's asked me to come along at the end of the month, when she has her murder mystery party. I'd just like to get a picture of the place in my head in advance.'

She shot me a quizzical look. 'Would you mind if I ask in what capacity you've been invited? She told me you're a guest, but

I just wondered whether the fact that you're a private investigator has something to do with it.'

'It's very nice of her to tell you to think of me as a guest, but what she really wants is for me to play the part of a detective in the murder mystery event. Apparently, I've been recommended to her by a mutual friend. It's good to think that thirty years in the murder squad haven't been for nothing. Tell me, have you been involved with a murder mystery event before?'

She shook her head and smiled. 'No, but I bet it's going to be enjoyable. She can be a lot of fun, you know. She's not an easy person to work for, not because she's unpleasant – far from it – but because she's not good at delegating. I ask her if she's got anything for me, stuff to type up, calls to make, emails to send, or things that she wants me to go and get for her, but she insists on doing everything herself – apart from running errands. She tells me to go sightseeing almost every day, and then in the evenings, we sit down together and talk about what I've seen. She's very keen to keep a low profile over here so she hardly ever leaves the island. I suppose when you're a household name with such a recognisable face, it's good to have a private bolthole. She's multi-talented. Did you know she's been writing a book?'

'Really? What sort of book?'

She shook her head again. 'I haven't a clue. I've never seen it, she never talks about it, she never asks me to do any research for her. I only know she's writing it because she insists on printing everything off at the end of the day, and I've seen the pile of pages. I don't think she trusts computers to save her work, so she has a printed manuscript that she adds to day by day and keeps locked away in the safe. According to a friend of mine at UCLA, the word on the street over there is that she's writing a tell-all autobiography, which could be interesting, possibly explosive. After over forty years in the business, I bet she knows all manner of potentially embarrassing secrets. I've been assuming that's what she's been writing but, for all I know, it might even be a thriller or a murder mystery.'

'What about her acting career? Is she still working?'

'Yes, but not at the moment. She's taking a few months off, but she's told me there's a new series of the Elisa Banbury mysteries coming up. That's being filmed partly in the UK and partly in the US, so we'll be heading over there in early September.' She shot me a little grin. 'I'm really looking forward to travelling with her – private jets, limos, five-star hotels. It promises to be exciting.'

'I'm sure you'll love it, but I'm surprised she isn't giving you more to do. Maybe that'll start up when you both go travelling. When she interviewed you for your job, surely she must have given you some idea of what your duties would be?'

She laughed. 'My interview was a glitzy dinner with her and Claire at The Ritz in London. She talked more about the food and the dress sense – or, rather, the lack of it – of the women sitting around us than about work. In between signing autographs for random people, she told me she's always had a personal assistant, and as her last PA left at Easter, she wanted a replacement, but she didn't go into any detail of what she wanted me to do.'

'Can I ask who Claire is?'

'She was my tutor when I was at Cambridge and she's become a close friend. She met Miss Graceland at a drinks do a few months back, and they hit it off. Miss Graceland told her she needed a PA who spoke Italian as well as English. Claire told her she thought I'd be perfect for the job, introduced me to her, and that's how I ended up here.'

Mary led me on a quick tour of the island, and it was as impressive as she had said. The buildings all around the inside of the massive defensive walls had been completely upgraded and turned into guest bedrooms, along with a gymnasium, a green-house and an amazing mini cinema with a massive screen and seating for a couple of dozen people. I followed Mary inside, where she pointed to a businesslike battery of computer equipment.

'I've been coming in here most days; there's been nothing else for me to do. It's amazing. She has access to thousands and thousands of films. Think of a movie, any movie, not just one of Miss Graceland's.'

'Um... how about *Star Wars*? It's a classic.'

Mary turned away and punched a few keys on a keyboard. Seconds later, the lights that had come on automatically as we entered the cinema now dimmed all by themselves and the screen came alive. The unmistakable theme music of the film boomed out of speakers all around us and the titles began to roll. It was an overwhelming onslaught on the senses and very, very impressive. We stood there in silence, eyes glued to the screen, for several minutes before Mary hit the keyboard again, the screen went dead, and the lights came back on.

'Quite something, eh? I may not have much work to do, but I'm going to come out of this job with an encyclopaedic knowledge of every movie ever made – not to mention every episode of the Elisa Banbury mysteries.'

* * *

I got back home just after six to find Anna looking worried. I had no doubt that I knew the reason, and it was nothing to do with my trip to Venice. While I repelled the boisterous welcome from Oscar, I went over to Anna and put my free arm around her shoulder.

'It'll be fine, Anna. Just you wait and see.'

She turned towards me and kissed me distractedly on the cheek. 'What if they don't like me?'

'Of course they'll like you. And I'm sure they'll love Tuscany as well.'

As I spoke, I muttered a silent prayer that the weekend would go smoothly. Anna and I had recently decided to get married, and I had had the bright idea of inviting my parents over from London for a few days so they could meet and get to know Anna. As the day of their arrival approached, I had been starting to question the wisdom of this decision. It promised to be complicated for a number of reasons. Firstly, my mum and dad were both in their eighties, secondly, they had never been to Italy before and didn't speak a word of the language, and, thirdly, but secretly most importantly, my mother had always had a very soft spot for Helen, my ex-wife. The two of them were still in regular contact, and every time I spoke to my mum on the phone, she insisted on making thinly veiled hints that the very best thing I could do would be to seek Helen out and try to make a go of it again. I had mentioned Anna to her a number of times, but the reaction had normally been little more than stony silence or an occasional grunt. I'm not as stupid as I look and I had thought it wisest not to mention this to Anna. She was worried enough as it was.

'What about the food? What if they don't like my cooking?'

Oscar must have heard the concern in Anna's voice because he dropped back onto all fours, moved over to her side and leant against her leg in a show of canine solidarity.

I did my best to offer support of my own. 'They'll love your cooking. I do, and I grew up in the house with them. My dad will eat anything – and he does.' I decided not to bring up his penchant for jellied eels, hurricane-strength vindaloo, tripe and onions, and worse. 'Mum's a little bit fussier, but as long as you don't use too much garlic, she'll be fine.'

Anna didn't look convinced. In fairness, neither was I. I told myself that worrying about it wouldn't help, so I helped myself to a cold beer from the fridge, poured a glass of white wine for Anna and led her outside into the shelter of my pergola. I had built this shortly after buying the little old house in the Tuscan hills just outside Florence a couple of years ago and I was very proud of my handiwork. It was now almost completely overgrown with a rambling rose, a luxuriant clematis, and two different vines. The result was an aromatic sunshade with bunches of green grapes hanging from it, already beginning to turn darker as they ripened. I sat down beside Anna and dissuaded Oscar from climbing onto our laps as we sipped our drinks and admired the view down over the vineyards and olive groves towards the valley of the River Arno below. It was a charming view, and I never tired of it. I reminded Anna of this in the hope that it would cheer her up a bit.

'Don't you worry. Mum and Dad's flight arrives at six on Friday, so we should be back here around this time, and I'm sure this view and a glass or two of the local wine will blow them away. Anyway, enough about Mum and Dad for now. Let me tell you about where I've been today.'

I gave her a brief description of Alice Graceland's island home – swearing her to secrecy – and she started to perk up. I told her that I would have to go and stay there for a couple of days at the end of the month with Oscar and, feeling sure that she, as a historian, would love Venice, I asked her if she would like to come with me. Alice Graceland hadn't mentioned whether I could bring a human as well as a canine companion, but I felt pretty sure that if I asked, she would say yes. At the same time, I was slightly hesitant to bring Anna because the last time she had got involved with one of my investigations, she had ended up having to spend a night in hospital with concussion. Although Miss Graceland's murder mystery weekend wasn't going to be a real investigation, it came as something of a relief when Anna declined the offer, telling me that she would use the days when Oscar and I were away to go and visit an old friend in the high Apennines, where the temperature would be refreshingly lower than it was likely to be here or in Venice.

After just a ham sandwich for dinner – I was still full from lunch – I took Oscar for a good walk up the hill. As usual, he covered about three times the distance that I did, chasing after sticks and pine cones that I lobbed into the olive groves for him to retrieve. As I walked, I thought back on the events of the day and my encounter with one of the best-known faces on the planet. I had been immensely impressed by how friendly – not to mention gorgeous – Alice Graceland had been, and how at the age of sixty-two, she appeared to be defying, if not reversing, the ageing process. I paused for thought – I was fifty-eight and that's perilously close to the big six-oh, so it wouldn't be that long before I, too, entered my seventh decade of existence, but I knew that ever achieving outstanding beauty was a forlorn hope for me. I hoped for Miss Graceland's sake that the murder mystery weekend would go well. I had distinctly got the feeling that she was trying to prove a point in the face of the predominantly male environment in which she had lived and worked for the last forty-five years. Hopefully, I would be able to play my part in helping her achieve this.

5

WEEKEND WITH THE PARENTS

I picked Mum and Dad up from Florence airport at a quarter to seven on Friday. Their flight was on time, and I had been expecting them to emerge sooner, but it was only when the doors from Customs control opened to finally reveal them that I realised why. My mother was in a wheelchair, being pushed by a young woman in uniform, and this came as an unwelcome shock to me. I hadn't seen them since before Christmas and, although I knew she'd been slowing down a bit, I hadn't realised to what extent. I hurried over to greet them and I was greatly relieved to see her push herself up out of the chair, thank the young woman and take half a dozen determined steps towards me. The first thing she said to me was predictably Mum.

'Daniel, you've lost weight. You're not eating enough.' She has always called me Daniel, and there's no way I'll ever get her to change now.

I held out my arms and gave her a hug before looking across at my dad, who was standing slightly behind her with the two bags.

'Hi, Mum, hi, Dad.' He and I shook hands. He's very English

about things like hugging, but he looked genuinely pleased to see me, as I was to see him. 'The van's only a short walk from here. Let me take the bags, Dad, and you can look after Mum.'

This produced an immediate response from her. 'I don't need looking after. All this wheelchair nonsense was ridiculous. Just because I was walking a bit slowly.' She was blustering for my benefit, but there was no getting away from the fact that she had aged quite a lot since I'd last seen her, and I felt a twinge of guilt for not having made the effort to go over to London to see them.

Dad caught my eye and winked at me as he laid a comforting hand on Mum's arm. 'It's all right, dear, you can walk as much as you like now.'

She replied stiffly, 'And I intend to.' But I noticed that she let Dad keep a supporting hand on her arm as we walked out into the evening sunshine.

It took less than half an hour to get back to my house, and I did my best to point out a few places of interest on the way, but the suburbs of Florence are far less appealing than the breathtaking beauty of the *centro storico*. As I picked my way through the heavy evening traffic, we talked – or, rather, Mum and I talked while Dad sat on the seat behind her and added only a few comments every now and then. He's never been a great talker, but Mum has always made up for that. At last, we turned off the main road and I headed up the much narrower lane winding its way up the hill to the village of Montevolpone and onwards towards my house. When we reached the village, I pointed out the church and the little piazza – there's not much else in Montevolpone – and then carried on uphill. Leaving the village, the road deteriorated into a white gravel track between the vineyards and olive groves, and I could see a cloud of dust being thrown up behind us as we crunched over the *strada bianca* and bumped through a few potholes.

I pulled up in front of my little stone house and went around to collect their bags from the boot. As I did so, Oscar came bounding out of the front door, tail wagging. When he saw that I was not alone, he skidded to a halt and studied them carefully for a few moments before deciding that they were friends and trotting over to say hello. Dad's definitely a dog person, but Mum has always been a bit scared – as a result of a nasty experience with a terrier when she was a girl – and we never had one in the house. Dad clicked his tongue and crouched down remarkably agilely to stroke Oscar while Mum stopped and shot me an uncertain look.

'My, he's a big dog...'

I hastened to reassure her. 'Yes, but he's very friendly and he likes ladies. You'll see.'

Bang on cue, Oscar stepped back from Dad and wandered over, tail wagging slowly, to greet my mother. Mum reached down hesitantly and patted him on the head. Oscar then surprised me by doing something I'd never seen him do before. He sat down primly in front of her and held up one paw towards her as if to shake her hand. Reassured, Mum shook his paw, gave him another pat on the head, and murmured, 'Good dog.'

Oscar glanced across at me for a moment, and I swear he winked. I gave a surreptitious sigh of relief. That was the first hurdle overcome.

No sooner had the thought occurred to me when the other hurdle appeared at the front door. Anna came out with a welcoming smile on her face, looking absolutely gorgeous in what might have been a new summer frock. At least, I couldn't remember ever having seen her wear it before, but I'm no expert on women's fashions – or, indeed, men's.

I made the introductions. 'Mum, Dad, this is Anna, my fiancée.'

I realised that I was actually holding my breath for a few

moments as Anna approached, but I was greatly relieved to see Mum take two steps forward, carefully avoiding tripping over Oscar, and hold out her arms towards Anna.

'Hello, my dear. I'd like to say that we've heard so much about you from Daniel, but he never was much good at remembering to phone home.' She gave Anna a hug and I started breathing again. Anna then turned towards Dad and, to my amazement, he held out his arms and gave her a hug as well, while I looked on in disbelief. Oscar sitting down and giving a paw, Dad spontaneously hugging somebody – what was the world coming to?

While Anna showed Mum around the house, I grabbed two bottles of cold beer and led Dad to my pergola, where we sat down to admire the view. It had been a hot day again – Florence can get stiflingly hot in summer – but this evening, there was just a hint of a breeze blowing, which made it very pleasant to be sitting outside while the sun dipped towards the horizon. I glanced over my shoulder to check that we weren't being overheard.

'How is Mum? I'm afraid the sight of her in a wheelchair came as a bit of a shock.'

He reached over and clinked his bottle against mine. 'She's not too bad, just slowing up a bit. There's talk of giving her a new hip, but you know her, she's not keen on any kind of operation. The doctor told her just to take it easy and see how it goes, but I've got a feeling she'll need to have the op sooner or later.'

'And you, Dad? You still look the same.'

He grinned at me. 'Just a few more aches and pains. Not too bad for eighty-four. You're looking well and Anna's a cracker. I'm really pleased to see you both looking so happy.' He sat back and stretched his legs, transferring his attention to the panorama before us. 'This is quite some place you have here. What a view! A bit different from Croydon.'

'My whole life is different now, and I wouldn't change back for anything. This place is great and Anna's wonderful.'

There was a movement at my feet and I felt Oscar's nose nudge my leg.

'And Oscar is great as well. He's a real part of the family now and, believe it or not, he's even helped me in some of my investigations.'

'How is the investigation business going?' There might even have been a hint of longing in his voice. Although Dad had spent his working life selling lawn mowers and other garden implements, he'd always been hooked on murder mysteries. It had been his enthusiasm for Agatha Christie – on his advice, I had read every single book of hers by the time I was fifteen – that had contributed in no small part towards my decision to join the police.

'Remarkably well, thanks.'

'Is it better than being a copper?'

'That's a good question.' I had a sip of beer while I considered my answer. 'The best thing about it is that I'm my own boss and, within reason, I now work fairly sensible hours. You and I both know that one of the main reasons Helen and I broke up was the fact that she hardly ever saw me. Nowadays, apart from exceptional circumstances, I'm normally home by six or seven at the latest. Apart from anything else, my four-legged friend here needs his evening walks. If I have a regret, it's that a lot of my time is spent with some pretty stupid, trivial matters.' I caught his eye for a moment. 'As I'm sure you can imagine, cases of marital infidelity make up the lion's share of my work. Still, I've got a good friend who's the head of the murder squad here in Florence and I sometimes get called in to help him with the more serious stuff.' I took another sip of beer and beamed at him. 'So, all in all, I have no regrets.'

We were interrupted by my phone. I shot Dad an apologetic glance and answered it. It was none other than the man in question – Virgilio.

'*Ciao*, Dan. Lina tells me you're going to Venice next weekend. I don't suppose you could do me a favour while you're there, could you?'

Virgilio is a very close friend, and I was quick to agree. 'By all means. Is it business or pleasure?'

'Pleasure. It's Lina's birthday in a couple of weeks, and for once, I've remembered and I even know what I want to give her. The problem is that it's a piece of glass from the island of Murano in the Venice lagoon, and it's very fragile. If I get them to send it by post or courier, I have a horrible feeling it'll arrive here in pieces. Seeing as you're going up there, could I arrange for somebody to give you the vase and then you bring it back for me? I have a good friend up there who says she can pick it up and let you have it. Would that be okay?'

'Of course it would. Just give me the details of where and when to meet your friend and I'll happily bring it back to Florence wrapped in my dirty washing. You're an old romantic at heart, aren't you?'

'I think we both know the answer to that one but, at least, that might make up for my forgetting Lina's birthday last year.'

At that moment, Mum and Anna appeared, so I rang off and hurried inside to fetch a bottle of cold white wine, a couple of glasses and a plate of nibbles. Anna had prepared bite-sized pieces of traditional Tuscan bruschetta, some topped with chopped tomatoes, some with soft goat's cheese and some with pâté. I poured the wine for Anna and Mum and sat down at the table under the pergola with them. I kept a close eye on both of their faces and I was unable to spot any signs of awkwardness so, hopefully, all was well so far.

We chatted increasingly easily. Anna told them about her job as a university lecturer and I gave them an edited version of some of my recent cases, including my trip to Venice – deliberately not mentioning Alice Graceland by name. This had the effect of stimulating my father to join in the conversation more than he normally did, and he sounded genuinely fascinated by what I'd been doing. In return, I got news via Mum that my brother had been promoted at long last – he's in insurance – and that both his children were doing well at university. Mum, who knows everything about the area in Croydon where they've lived ever since I was a boy, told me about various friends, some doing well and some not so well. It sounded very parochial now, and I found myself yet again thanking my lucky stars that I'd chosen to take the big decision to give up my career with the police and move here to this idyllic spot. Meeting up with Oscar and Anna had been the icing on the cake. I sat back and admired the view, knowing that I was a lucky man.

'Daniel? Daniel, have you been listening? I bet you haven't heard a word I've said.' My mother's voice roused me from my thoughts, and I saw her turn to Anna with an air of exasperation. 'I can always tell, you know. He gets that faraway look in his eyes when he goes into detective mode. He was like it as a little boy. Has he told you about the Sherlock Holmes Club?'

I was definitely listening now and I tried to intervene, but it was too late. I could see a twinkle in Anna's eyes as my mother set out to embarrass me in front of her – and she succeeded. 'When he was twelve, he and a couple of other boys in the road decided that they were going to be detectives. They used to go around hunting for clues to solve crimes.' She glanced across at me and smiled as she must have seen my cheeks colouring. 'We had the mystery of the dead mouse, the mystery of the broken milk bottle, the mystery of the missing shoe, and oh-so many more mysteries.'

Anna was positively beaming by this time. 'The mystery of the dead mouse? This I must hear. Let me guess, it was next-door neighbour's cat. Surely you should have got that. Am I right?'

As my professional reputation had been impugned, I felt I had to respond. 'That was what everybody thought at first, but we managed to prove the cat innocent.' I turned and pointed an accusing finger at my father. 'You have before you, ladies and gentlemen, the culprit. Would you please confess to Anna your part in this heinous crime?'

My dad was only too happy to play along. He adopted an expression of contrition as he confessed. 'I admit it. I was responsible.'

Anna was looking less sure of herself now. 'What did you do?'

Dad shook his head ruefully. 'I'm afraid the mouse must have been hiding under the wheel of my car. When I reversed out of the drive, the boys told me I must have killed it. I won't go into the rather disgusting detail of how they managed to prove that the mouse had been flattened by something heavy, but you get the picture.'

I turned triumphantly towards Anna. 'You see, without the intervention of the Sherlock Holmes Club, Tiddles next door might have been wrongfully accused.'

Anna was grinning as well now. 'And the rest is history. Fired with enthusiasm after the success of your first case, in which you proved the innocence of a poor feline, you knew how you wanted to spend the rest of your life. Am I right?'

I grinned back. 'Without the Tiddles saga, who knows what I might have ended up doing?'

6

NEXT FRIDAY MORNING

According to the regulations of the Italian state railways, dogs travelling on high-speed trains must be equipped with muzzles. Oscar didn't like the muzzle I had bought for him and, for my part, I felt almost embarrassed having to tie it on him. Fortunately, this was Italy, and there's a lovely Italian expression that translates roughly as, 'No sooner is the law made, than the way to get round it is invented.' The ticket collector who came walking through the carriage spotted him sitting at my feet, wearing his muzzle and looking fed up. She stopped to inform me that she was quite happy not only for me to remove his muzzle but also for him to sit on the empty leather seat alongside me so he could be more comfortable. He licked her hand gratefully and she went off with a smile.

I gave him a treat and apologised again for the demeaning muzzle. In reply, he licked my hand as well, and I got the impression that he understood and forgave me. As the train picked up speed and dived into an impressive series of tunnels bored through the Apennine mountains, I sat back and reflected on the past few days with my parents. All in all, things couldn't have gone much better. Within a very short space of time, Mum and Anna had ganged up against me and had soon been giggling like schoolgirls at embarrassing tales of my youth. They had spent hours in the kitchen, where they had swapped recipes, and I had found myself served Yorkshire pudding for the first time in ages. Most importantly, Mum had never once brought up the subject of Helen, my ex-wife, and I was feeling very relieved as a result.

Dad and I had taken Oscar for walks in the hills, where Dad was fascinated by all the different plants, from olive trees and vines to wild rosemary and orchids. He loves his garden and he appeared fascinated by my new plant identification app on my phone. This had been a Christmas present from Lina, and it was surprisingly accurate. All I had to do was point it at a plant, and it would produce the Latin name and, with the more familiar ones, the common name. I offered to buy him one but, as his idea of a phone is a nineteen-sixties vintage landline, he had nothing on which to instal it. I wondered whether maybe I should buy him a smartphone for Christmas, but I had a feeling it would lie unused in the back of a drawer. Technology never was his forte and, as for my mum, she believes the Internet to be the work of the Devil.

We went into Florence to see the sights on a number of occasions, including taking Mum and Dad to visit the Uffizi gallery. We had to book in advance and there were crowds of people in there, admiring some of the most famous paintings in the world, but they both seemed to enjoy themselves in spite of all the visitors. We walked across the Ponte Vecchio and, inevitably, called in at the office of Dan Armstrong, Private Investigations. Mum did a lot more walking than I had expected, and she managed pretty well although, come the evenings, I could see that she was weary.

When the time came to take them back to the airport on

Tuesday, both Mum and Anna had been in tears, and I had felt an overwhelming sensation of relief that Anna had been accepted into the family – as had Oscar. Mum had actually hugged him before she left and promised to bring him 'something special' next time she came to see him. All in all, things had gone a whole lot more smoothly than I had been expecting – apart from the numerous revelations about the Sherlock Holmes Club, of course, which still made Anna snigger when she spoke of them. I had little doubt that before long, she would tell Lina and she, of course, would then tell Virgilio. As a result, I felt sure the next time I had to visit the Florence murder squad offices at the *questura*, I would be the object of considerable ridicule. Still, the important thing was that by the time that I dropped my parents back to the airport, I had been confident that all was well on the family front.

The train arrived in Venice on time and, as before, Mary was waiting for me on the platform. Oscar greeted her enthusiastically – no surprise there – and she appeared equally pleased to meet him. As we walked out of the station, we chatted.

'I've prepared the final list of guests – Miss Graceland has a copy for you – and there are going to be twelve in total: two big-name directors, two producers, an agent, a couple of other studio staff – I'm not too sure what they do – and two actors whose names I'm sure you'll recognise. Would you believe Dirk Foster and Lucy O'Connell?' She caught my eye. 'Movie royalty, right?'

I nodded in agreement. I had seen a couple of films featuring Foster. He was a Sylvester Stallone lookalike with bulging muscles in places where most normal humans like me don't have places. As for Lucy O'Connell, she had been acclaimed as the sexiest woman on the planet some years ago with her pouting lips and gravity-defying bust. I hadn't heard much about her recently. I seemed to remember reading that she had been in trouble of some sort, but the detail escaped me. She was certainly a big name though, and I looked forward to meeting her – along with Foster and his muscles.

I queried Mary's maths. 'I make that nine. Who are the others?'

'Three partners, then there's you and me, along with the actors for the murder mystery event, although they won't be staying over. Add in Valentina, Diego and their daughter, and that'll be over twenty people. I think Miss Graceland's quiet island retreat is going to get busy.'

As we emerged into the sunlight, I saw Diego in the launch. As before, he was waiting a little way out in the channel and when he spotted us, he came chugging over to the steps. Oscar's eyes lit up as we approached the Grand Canal. Like most Labradors, he loves water, and I made sure I kept a tight hold on his lead to prevent him from diving in. Apart from the risk of being run down by one of the numerous vessels travelling up and down the waterway, I had read that swimming was prohibited – maybe because the waters were potentially polluted – and I didn't want him to catch anything.

This time, Mary kindly asked Diego to take a different route so that I could see more of the city, and we headed off in the opposite direction. After passing underneath a distinctly modern-looking curved footbridge, we turned left into a narrower canal. The buildings here were far from medieval, and it was clear that this was a more modern, predominantly commercial area, and I even spotted a few cars and vans driving alongside us for a while.

A few minutes later, we emerged from the canal into a much wider waterway with the long island of Giudecca to our right and a line of superyachts moored to our left alongside quays that were a reminder – if one were needed – of Venice's illustrious past as a naval power. Ahead of us was the long, low outline of the Lido and, between us and it, the *Isola dei Cigni*. Sight of Alice Graceland's island brought me back to why I was here, and I turned towards Mary, who was sitting stroking Oscar's ears, a blissful expression on his face.

We had gone into the cabin to get out of the burning sun, and I was sitting opposite Mary on one of the smart, red-cushioned benches. 'Am I right in thinking that the only way to get to Miss Graceland's island is by private boat? It's not on a regular bus stop, is it?' I stopped and corrected myself. 'Sorry, not bus, boat.'

'We're not that far from the main route taken by the *vaporetti* – that's the name the locals give to the passenger ferries – going to and from the Lido, but none of them stop at the island. So, yes, you either need your own boat or you take a water taxi.'

'This may be a stupid question, but how deep is the water around the island?'

'I've no idea, but it's certainly deep enough for fairly big ships to come past not that far off the island.'

'As a means to get away from the paparazzi, it's a perfect solution. I wonder if Miss Graceland will stay here indefinitely.'

'It wouldn't surprise me. On the occasions when she's spoken about her past, I've definitely got the impression that her career hasn't all been plain sailing, in spite of her phenomenal success. I wouldn't be at all surprised if there are quite a few skeletons in her cupboard that she would be happy to leave behind and never see again.' She paused for a moment's reflection. 'She probably deserves a bit of peace and quiet – and I can't think of many better places to do that than an island in the Venice lagoon.'

'She told me she'd had a fractious relationship with the media. I couldn't find a social media presence for her. I would have thought you'd handle that sort of thing for her.'

'That was one of the first things I offered to do, but she was dead against it. She's quite old-fashioned about that sort of thing, even though she looks and sounds so youthful.'

I reflected on what Mary had said. Alice Graceland's career had been meteoric, but success probably hadn't come as easily as one might assume. Social media can be brutal, and I didn't blame her one bit for choosing to steer clear of it. Maybe her choice of a fortress on an island had not been by chance. As Mary had said, here, amid the beauty of the Venice lagoon, she should be able to relax – or at least she would be able to, once this murder mystery weekend was over.

* * *

I found Alice Graceland in her blissfully cool office, sitting at her desk. This time, her laptop was open, and I couldn't miss a pile of printed A4 sheets, probably an inch deep, alongside it on the desktop. I'm not a betting man but I would have put money on this turning out to be the manuscript of the book she was writing, whatever it was. She looked up and smiled as I walked in, and her smile broadened as she spotted Oscar. She jumped to her feet and came around to shake my hand and crouch down in front of my very happy Labrador to make a fuss of him.

She glanced up at me with a delighted smile on her face that mirrored the toothy canine smile on his. 'Hello again. What a lovely dog. And he's the famous Oscar, isn't he? Yes, you're a very good boy, aren't you? Oh, yes, you are.'

I assumed that the last bit of her comment was directed at Oscar and I wondered idly how she had known his name, so I responded to the first part. 'Good morning, Miss Graceland. It's Oscar all right. He's almost four years old, and I think I can safely assure you that he's your friend for life now. Of course, a fillet steak would probably help your chances of being included in his top ten favourite people, but I think you're pretty well there already.' From the way his tail was wagging, I had little doubt about the veracity of this.

'Do, please, call me Alice. "Miss Graceland" makes me feel so old. Your name's Dan, isn't it? Dan and Oscar, the crime-solving duo – that's what Selena calls you, so I'll do the same.'

I did my best to act as if being on first-name terms with two of the most famous and most beautiful women on the planet was nothing out of the ordinary for me. 'Thank you, Alice. Oscar and I are at your service.'

Today, she was wearing a pair of white shorts and a pink, linen blouse. Around her neck was a thin, gold chain with a little capital 'A' studded with diamonds suspended from it. Her mass of light-blonde hair, which had been tied back the previous time I had seen her, was now hanging loose around her shoulders. She had looked ten or twenty years younger than her real age last time we'd met, and she looked even younger today. Ungenerously, I wondered to what extent this might be due to surgical assistance, but that was none of my business. She looked great – and in her profession, appearance counts for a lot.

'Mary said you'd got a list of names for me.'

She pointed over her shoulder to the desktop. 'It's just there on the corner of my desk.'

While she remained apparently enchanted by Oscar – and I could see that it was mutual – I walked over to the desk and located the printed list. As I did so, my eyes strayed across to the pile of pages on the other side of the laptop. I felt pretty sure that this was the manuscript Mary had mentioned, but all I could read was a single word on the top sheet, presumably the title: *Payback*. I didn't want to appear nosey, so I retrieved the list of names and returned to where Alice was still crouching down with Oscar. The title of the book – if, indeed, that was what I'd seen – fascinated me. Was it a murder mystery, was it a thriller or, as Mary had surmised, was it Alice Graceland's autobiography? And if it was the latter, who was trying to get revenge against whom? And for what?

Any further conjecture was interrupted as Alice stood up again and pointed at the list in my hands.

'There are going to be nine guests, and three of them are bringing their companions.'

The sarcastic way she pronounced the word 'companions' prompted my first question. 'Would that be wives or husbands?'

Reluctantly, she abandoned Oscar and walked over to one of the sofas, indicating that I should take a seat opposite her. I did as instructed and it came as no surprise to see Oscar position himself alongside her with his nose on her knees, staring adoringly into her eyes. She started stroking him again as she answered my question. 'A wife, a girlfriend, and a toyboy.'

I glanced down at the list of twelve names and ran through them. I recognised the actors, Dirk Foster and Lucy O'Connell, but not all of the others. Desmond Norman, the famous producer, was there, along with Carlos Rodriguez and Wilfred Baker, who were well-known film directors. The other seven names were new to me. Most were men, but there was a woman whose name was unfamiliar to me – Maggie McBride – along with her plus one, indicated as Rocco Gentile. I shot Alice a cryptic look.

'Would I be right in thinking that Mr Gentile is the guest you describe as a toyboy? What makes you call him that? Have you met him before?'

She rolled her eyes. 'I haven't met this particular incarnation, but I know the type. Maggie's the same age as I am – although she'd never admit it to you – but she has a hankering for men half her age – with a definite penchant for tattoos, medallions and skintight jeans.'

'I see. And do the guests all know each other?'

'I've known all of them for quite some time, and most of them know – or know of – each other. I like one or two of them a lot and the others not so much.'

I reflected on that last remark. I couldn't work out why she should have chosen to invite people if she didn't like them. If it turned out that Alice Graceland really was writing her autobiography, I couldn't help wondering whether any of this weekend's guests would get a mention in the text. If so, would that be complimentary or less so? After all, with a title like *Payback*, the book might well end up ruffling quite a few feathers. It seemed unlikely that she would invite guests to her party if she didn't like them, but stranger things have happened. Of course, I reminded myself, I might be barking up the wrong tree completely. *Payback* struck me as quite a good title for a thriller as well. As for barking dogs, Oscar had by now subsided onto the floor alongside his new best friend and was lying on his back, all four paws in the air, his tail sweeping the spotless marble floor as he lay there.

Alice looked up from him. 'I told you I would write him into the plot for tomorrow night, didn't I? I thought he would make a good sniffer dog. What do you think?'

'Yes, he's good at sniffing stuff out.' I could have added that he was best at sniffing food and other dogs' backsides, but I left it at that for now.

The famous actor continued to stroke my happy Labrador as she gave me my instructions. 'The actors for the murder mystery are coming this evening at six. I trust you'll be able to make it.'

'Of course. If it's all right with you, I'll give Oscar a little walk around the island first and then I need to pop back into town quickly to see somebody on behalf of a friend of mine in Florence.'

She looked up. 'You're not thinking of bringing them here, are you? I'd rather not have any more people wandering around, trampling my plants. This weekend's going to be bad enough.'

'Don't worry, I'm just picking up a parcel for a friend. I won't be away for long and I certainly won't mention that you're here.'

I toyed with the idea of asking her what she was writing but then decided that this, just like her efforts to reverse the ageing process, was none of my business, so I returned to the matter in hand.

'When are the guests arriving?'

'Mary has the details, but I believe most are arriving tomorrow in the course of the morning, in time for lunch. She'll show you to your room now, if you like.' She finally relinquished Oscar, stood up and gave me some unexpected and unwelcome news. 'If it isn't there already, you'll be getting your costume later today.'

'You want me to dress up?' I hadn't been expecting this and I had a sinking feeling as the thought struck home. Her answer did nothing to reassure me.

'We're all going to dress up.' She caught my eye. 'Don't worry, Valentina tells me she's confident your costume will fit – she made it after seeing you last week. I'd like you to wear it this evening when the actors come. We're going to have a full dress rehearsal.'

The sinking feeling had just about reached my feet by now. 'Dressed up as what?'

'What do you think? Here in Venice, it has to be *Carnevale* characters. Renaissance clothes, masks, lots of silk, lace and tassels.'

For Venetians, the February carnival is the high spot of the year, with glittering events, parties, carnival processions on land and water, and the famous masked balls where people travel from all over the world to don masks and join in the celebrations.

I stifled a sigh. With a fiancée who lived and breathed the Middle Ages and the Renaissance, I had already found myself being squeezed – and I do mean squeezed – into tights and pantaloons on several occasions in the past and I was under no illusions as to how ridiculous I looked. Still, it sounded as though I didn't have any choice, so I took a deep breath and accepted my fate with as much grace as I could muster.

'That sounds great. Thank you.'

7

FRIDAY AFTERNOON

I found Mary sitting on the terrace and I followed Oscar – once I'd been able to persuade him to abandon Alice Graceland – as he trotted across to renew his acquaintance with Mary. She looked up as she saw me approach. 'Did you get the guest list?'

'Yes, thanks, and I recognise the names of some of them, but not all. For instance, who's Maggie McBride?'

'She's the widow of Caspar McBride, the oil billionaire. Since he died years ago, she's been involved in the production – by which I mean the financing – of numerous big-budget movies.' She shot me a grin. 'According to Miss Graceland, very few movies get made these days without Maggie McBride's approval or participation. When it comes to movie producers, you don't get much bigger than that.'

'Unless you're Desmond Norman.'

'Quite. These two are arguably the most important producers in Hollywood today.'

'Alice Graceland definitely knows the right people.' Mary nodded in agreement and I glanced down at the list again. 'There are a few other names I didn't recognise. Who are Jack Sloane and Greg Gupta?'

'Jack Sloane occupies legendary status in Hollywood, but he isn't that well known outside that world. He's a talent scout and, in the course of his career, he's been casting director for some of the biggest film companies and responsible for discovering some of the biggest stars in the movie world today. When I was writing my thesis, I made a special study of him and one of the things I discovered is that there's a saying in Hollywood that his cell phone number is one of the most closely guarded secrets in the universe – far more secret than the recipe for Coca-Cola or the existence of aliens among us. If Jack picks you, you go far, so the queue of hopefuls outside his door goes around the block two or three times.'

'And Greg Gupta?'

'He's one of the most popular scriptwriters of the moment and very successful. He and Carlos Rodriguez, the director, are a couple.'

'I see.' I glanced down the list of names again. 'And what about Alastair Groves and his wife? Their names aren't familiar to me.'

'He's an interesting choice.' Mary took a surreptitious glance around, but we were alone. 'He's an agent, a theatrical agent. He represented Miss Graceland for a number of years back at the start of her career, until they parted company a long time ago.'

'And she has a different agent nowadays?'

'Yes, for over twenty years, but he isn't coming this weekend.'

'Funny that Miss Graceland should choose to invite her former agent, but not her current one.'

Mary nodded again. 'I thought the same thing, but maybe she's on a nostalgia trip. Who knows? She didn't tell me.'

I stood there and took stock. 'From what I can see of this list, and from what you've been telling me, if a bomb were to drop on this island tomorrow, the movie industry could potentially be crippled.'

'They're certainly all major players. No question about that.' She stroked Oscar's head and then stood up. 'Would you like me to show you to your room? And then I can show you around the island in a bit more detail than last time, if you like.'

I agreed willingly, and we set off along the brick path that circled the gardens. As we walked past the single-storey buildings set against the walls, she pointed out the guest bedrooms and told me that if I wanted, she would be able to give me a printout in the morning of which had been allocated to which guests. I've always had a curious streak, so I said yes, please. She took me right along the line of bedrooms to the very last door and opened it.

'Room twelve, this is yours. You should be very comfortable, but if there's anything you need, just ask me or Valentina. Let me give you my phone number and hers.'

After exchanging phone numbers with her, I stepped inside and had to agree that the room looked most comfortable. It was bigger than I had expected and somebody – probably Valentina – had even been kind enough to lay out a big, folded blanket alongside the bed for my four-legged friend. The floor had been freshly tiled with light-grey marble slabs, and hefty wooden beams supported the pristine, white-painted ceiling, giving the room an almost rustic air. The conversion had obviously been done with considerable taste, and a quick glance into the bathroom showed me yet more marble and glistening white bathroom furniture. I looked back at Mary, who was standing by the door.

'This looks wonderful. Thank you so much and do, please,

say thank you to Valentina. With a dozen guests coming – plus me – she must be working all hours.'

'Gabriella, her daughter, was here working with her all day yesterday and she's back today along with Guido, their boy. Miss Graceland says they make a most efficient team.'

'Do Valentina and Diego live here on the island?'

She nodded. 'They have a cottage over there on the far side, alongside my apartment.'

'And their son and daughter?'

'They both live in Mestre, on the mainland.' She elaborated. 'They've been telling me that most ordinary Venetians have been squeezed out of the city because property values and rents have gone through the roof.'

I left my bag in the room, followed her out and we continued our tour. A bit further along was the gym and, beyond it, a large, old greenhouse filled with plants. So luxuriant was the vegetation in there, I could hardly see from one end to the other and I couldn't recognise even half of what looked like exotic plants. I decided if I had a bit of spare time, I would come back with my new plant identification app and see just how true its boast of being able to identify 95 per cent of the world's flora really was.

As I turned away, Mary gave me a few words of explanation. 'Miss Graceland spends quite a lot of time pottering around the garden. She's very interested in plants and flowers. You maybe noticed that she's got a whole shelf of books on plants and gardening in her study.'

I looked across towards the central part of the island and had to admire the variety of trees and plants on display in the gardens. Although the Venice region can get very cold in winter, presumably the surrounding water meant that the island bene-fitted from its own microclimate, and this accounted for the presence of palm trees, cactus and a charming little grove of lemon trees, heavy with fruit.

We walked across the luxuriant lawn until we reached the swimming pool, and I was relieved to find that this was fenced off. I felt sure that the lure of the water would have been too much for Oscar to resist, and having a soggy, wet dog around the place probably wouldn't have endeared me to Alice Graceland.

Mary pointed out what she called the cottage, inhabited by Diego and Valentina. This was a good-sized building, also built up against the perimeter wall, and alongside it was the smaller construction where Mary told me she had her quarters. As I looked around, I could see no fewer than eight different sets of stone steps leading up to the ramparts and I decided to go up and investigate. At this point, Mary excused herself, telling me she felt she had better check in with Alice on the off chance that she might have something for her to do before lunch. This reminded me of something I'd been meaning to ask.

'Last time I was here, I had lunch with Miss Graceland in the dining room, but I wouldn't want to disturb her again. Is there somewhere else I can get something to eat?'

'Yes, of course. I'm sorry, I should have said. Valentina told me to ask you to join her, Diego and me in the kitchen. I sometimes have lunch with them and we normally eat at twelve-thirty.'

'What about Miss Graceland? Does she normally eat alone?'

'Occasionally, although she often asks me to join her – not for work, just to chat, mainly about me rather than her. I enjoy her company but I always come away hungry. Her normal diet is what she calls "rabbit food". You can probably imagine what that consists of.'

'When I was here earlier in the month, she mentioned that big meals were an exception for her.'

'She interrupts her diet in exceptional circumstances, like

having lunch with you or, I'm sure, with her guests this weekend, but, otherwise, it's all carefully calorie controlled. She's told me that all her adult life, she's had to follow a strict dietary regime in order to keep looking good for the cameras.' She caught my eye and smiled ruefully. 'This celebrity business can have its downsides.'

She pointed out where the kitchens were situated, just along from the dining room, and then headed back in the direction of Alice's office, while Oscar and I climbed the nearest set of steps onto the top of the walls. From up here, it was clear to see just how massive the fortifications were. There was a walkway at least two metres wide with a brick wall taller than me on the seaward side, punctured every few metres by diamond-shaped portholes, some higher, some lower, no doubt designed for bow, cannon or musket fire. On the inside, there was no perimeter wall at all, just a three-metre drop to the ground below. I kept a watchful eye on Oscar, but he didn't demonstrate any inclination to fling himself off, so I relaxed and put my face to one of the portholes. The view was exceptional.

I found myself looking back towards Venice. The smooth waters of the lagoon were a light grey-blue, the sky not dissimilar in colour, and Venice itself was a long, low pink and white line bisecting the scene. Through the heat haze, I thought I could even just about make out the peaks of the Dolomites in the far distance. Rising up among the red roofs of Venice, I counted no fewer than five belltowers and the domes and roofs of six churches, including the white mass of the cathedral with the Palazzo Ducale alongside it.

To my surprise, the view was punctuated by numerous trees and patches of greenery. I couldn't remember seeing more than an occasional shrub on the way over, but obviously, I hadn't been looking in the right direction. I stood there and tried to imagine myself as a soldier on the lookout for enemy ships belonging to Venice's mortal enemy, the other great Italian maritime power, the Republic of Genoa, back in the fourteenth century when the fortress had been constructed. Anna had researched the island for me; having a historian as a fiancée can be useful.

I did a complete circuit of the ramparts with Oscar and by the time I got back around to my original starting point, I had a pretty clear idea in my head of the geography of the fortress. Roughly half of the interior wall space had buildings butting up against it, with their sloping roofs starting just below the level of the walkway. The largest of the buildings, where Alice had her office and living quarters, was closest to the main entrance, while the dining room and kitchen were just a bit further along from there.

Apart from Valentina and Diego's cottage alongside Mary's place on the far side, all the principal accommodation roughly formed a banana shape, while the rest of the island was taken up with the garden with the pool in the centre.

A glance at my watch told me that it was almost twelve-thirty. 'Right, then, Oscar, it's lunchtime.'

Without a moment's hesitation, he turned and headed down the steps. When it comes to food, his comprehension is second to none.

8

FRIDAY AFTERNOON

Oscar and I received a warm welcome from Valentina and her daughter, both of them wearing businesslike aprons. We sat around a fine old wooden table at one end of the long kitchen, and I was delighted to find that this room was also air-conditioned. The temperature outside had been steadily climbing, and Oscar wasn't the only one who was panting by the time we got inside. I spared a thought for the hordes of tourists struggling to take in the sights of this unique city under these conditions. I couldn't see a thermometer, but I felt sure that the temperature outside had to be well into the thirties by now.

I was relieved to find that lunch was less copious than the meal I had had with Alice last time. Considering that I was going to be staying for three days, this was probably for the best, unless I was considering buying a whole new wardrobe. I sat at one end of the table, with Diego at the opposite end with his son, Guido, beside him. Valentina didn't bother with antipasti and produced a steaming bowl of pasta. Pasta comes in all shapes and sizes, and this variety looked like fat spaghetti, almost the thickness of drinking straws. She told me that this was a local speciality called *bigoli*, and she served it *alle vongole* – with clams – in a rich, brown sauce. She very kindly asked whether I thought Oscar might like some, and he nodded before I did.

I was introduced to Gabriella, Valentina's daughter, who looked as though she was in her late twenties. She was a cheerful-looking woman who told me that she worked for the Venice Tourist Board and she very quickly monopolised the conversation at table. In answer to a query from me, she reeled off a long list of festivities and festivals that took place here in Venice in the course of the year. These ranged from the world-famous *Carnevale* in February to a mind-boggling variety of historic regattas. At the mention of these, Diego, who had been sitting quietly at the end of the table, tucking into his pasta, suddenly perked up.

'My boy, Guido here, is taking part in the September regatta as part of a four-man gondola crew.'

I looked at Guido with interest. 'You're a gondolier?' He was probably only about twenty, but he had broad shoulders and strong forearms – no doubt a prerequisite for any gondolier.

He nodded. 'I'm still a trainee, but I've almost finished, and, if all goes well, I'll get my licence in time for the regatta.' He went on to tell me about the complexities of the course he had to follow – over and above the practical test of boat handling – including the history, art and culture of Venice, and even a smattering of important words and phrases in a number of different languages. I wondered cynically whether one of these important phrases might be, *Sorry it's so expensive.* On my way up from Florence in the train, out of curiosity, I had googled, *How much is a private gondola ride?* and the answer had been as much as a hundred euros for half an hour. On this basis, it looked as though being a gondolier paid a whole lot better than being a private investigator – but my job was probably less tiring on the arms.

After the delicious pasta, Valentina served a local speciality: salt cod and polenta. Polenta, made from maize, has never ranked particularly highly on my list of favourite dishes, but this was different and exceptional. She explained that the dried cod, preserved in salt barrels the old way as it had been back in the days before refrigerators, had been soaked in milk for hours to soften it and remove the saltiness, then mixed into a smooth paste with olive oil and served on top of the polenta. I couldn't fault it and Oscar's eyes opened wide as he, too, was served a generous portion. I had brought a supply of dried dog food for him – occupying almost half my bag – but if he was going to be fed like this, I felt sure I would be taking quite a lot of his normal rations back home again.

I hadn't forgotten my errand to collect the glass vase for Virgilio, so I told them that I had to go back into town after lunch and asked how to get off the island.

Diego was quick to offer to help. 'I can drop you into town in the launch or, if you want to be more independent, you can take the little boat. The outboard motor is electric, and I can give you the key and show you how to start it. It's dead easy. Where are you going?'

'I have to meet somebody at Caffè Florian in Piazza San Marco at three. Do you know it?'

Valentina and her daughter looked impressed. 'Nothing but the best for you. Caffè Florian is famous the world over.'

This sounded good – and no doubt expensive.

Diego looked less impressed. 'There's nowhere you're allowed to moor up near there, so it'll be best if I take you in the launch, drop you off and pick you up again.' He shot me a hint of a smile.

'Even Venice has parking restrictions. I have to collect a package for Miss Graceland, as well as a couple of cases of fine wines from a wine merchant – Miss Graceland insists on giving her guests the best.'

This also sounded good.

Mary joined in. 'I'll come too, if you don't mind, Mr Armstrong. Not to the café, but I haven't been inside St Mark's Cathedral yet, so I can check that out while you have your meeting, and then I'll come back in the launch with you again. Is that all right?'

I gave her a smile. 'Of course it is, and please drop the "Mr Armstrong". My name's Dan.' I glanced around at the others. 'And that goes for all of you.'

After a couple of fresh apricots and a strong espresso, I went back to my room, where I spent the next hour or so checking out the list of guests that Alice Graceland had given me.

Desmond Norman's Wikipedia page told me he had just hit eighty-five, and the photo on the page didn't do him any favours. With his mop of white hair and his wrinkled face, he looked every one of his eighty-five years and maybe a bit more. Maggie McBride, on the other hand, although allegedly sixty-two like Alice, was photographed in a selection of very revealing gowns, dripping with gold, and she looked twenty years younger than her real age – at least from a distance. Alastair Groves, the theatrical agent, was a fit-looking man in his mid-seventies, while the photo of his wife, Sandra, reminded me of Maggie Smith's countess character in *Downton Abbey* – a real doyenne, dripping with gold and jewels and with a supercilious expression on her face.

Wilfred 'Freddie' Baker was a mere forty-three years old. He was described as a wunderkind, the youngest ever director of no fewer than three Oscar-winning movies. I couldn't find any mention of his girlfriend, Antoinette Latour, but I had a suspicion that I would find that she was younger and prettier than him. That appeared to be the way it worked in Hollywood.

Jack Sloane, the casting director and discoverer of movie stars, was a big man – both in height and girth. He was seventy-five years old and he, like Desmond Norman, hadn't aged well. Unlike Alice Graceland, he evidently hadn't discovered the elixir of eternal youth and, from the colour of his cheeks, I had a feeling his blood pressure was probably through the roof.

A photo of Greg Gupta clearly showed his Indian heritage. He was a slim man in his early fifties, with a fine head of black hair. Another man with a fine head of suspiciously dark hair was Gupta's partner, Carlos Rodriguez, the well-known director, who bore an uncanny resemblance to the actor who plays Zorro. Like many of the other guests, he was also past his seventieth birthday.

Setting aside my iPad, I took Oscar for a little walk around the garden and spotted Diego deadheading the roses in a flower bed. He looked up as I approached.

'Ready to go, Dan? It's half-past two and it'll take at least fifteen minutes to get to San Marco.'

'Yes, thanks. Are you sure it's convenient for you if we go now?'

'No problem. As I said, I have to go into town anyway. I'll call Mary and meet you at the launch.'

He headed back across to Mary's accommodation while Oscar and I wandered over towards the main entrance. The massive gate was open and we descended the ramp to the jetty and stood there, looking around. I had put Oscar on his lead and I kept a tight grip on my end of it just in case he were to consider diving in, but he seemed happy to stand there and sniff the gentle breeze. I was born and bred in London, and my experience of the sea is pretty limited. It felt totally alien to find myself in this environment where the roads are canals, the only way to get about is by boat, and people live on islands.

The trip back across the lagoon to San Marco took just over fifteen minutes, and Diego explained the strict speed limit in the lagoon. In Venice's narrow canals, the limit was no more than five kilometres per hour, little more than walking pace, for fear that the bow waves of passing boats might disturb the foundations of the surrounding properties. Anna had explained to me before I left home that almost all of the wonderful buildings in this unique city – including the duomo itself – weren't built on dry land or solid foundations, but on wooden piles, driven into the mud below. Little wonder the city was living on borrowed time.

Diego dropped Mary and me off alongside the gondola rank at the entrance to St Mark's square, and we instantly found ourselves in the midst of a mass of humanity. We arranged to meet back again in half an hour and Mary disappeared in the direction of the massive, white marble façade of the cathedral, while Oscar and I set off past the amazingly slim, tall belltower and into the piazza. How this managed to stay upright on foundations of wood was beyond me. As we threaded our way through the crowd, heading diagonally across the square to where the café was situated underneath a seemingly endless row of stone arches on the far side, I saw faces and heard voices from all over the globe.

I checked my watch and saw that it was exactly three o'clock and, in case I might have any doubts, bells all over the city began striking the hour. The arrangement Virgilio had made with his friend was that she would be sitting out in the square in front of the café with a cardboard box on her table. Almost all of the tables were taken, and it took me a few moments before I spotted the cardboard box on one right at the back. Oscar and I were already making our way in that direction when the woman with the box saw us and waved to attract our attention. Presumably, Virgilio had told her to look out for a man with a big, black dog. I waved back and walked up to her. She stood up as I approached and gave me a friendly smile.

'Dan? There can't be too many tall men with black Labradors walking around Piazza San Marco.' She was probably in her early forties and she had chestnut hair and a wedding ring on her left hand. Her eyes were emerald green and penetrating, and I had a feeling she didn't miss much.

I smiled back and held out my hand. 'And you must be Giulia.'

We shook hands, and I sat down alongside her, looking out onto the sea of tourists in the square, while Oscar gave Giulia a warm greeting. A very smart waiter wearing a white uniform with enough gold braid for an admiral of the fleet appeared at my shoulder and enquired what I would like to drink. Giulia had a little espresso in front of her, but I ordered an alcohol-free beer as it was so hot. Fortunately – or more probably, wisely – she had chosen a table in the shade, and I was glad of that – for Oscar's sake and for mine.

She pushed the cardboard box, the size of a shoebox, across the table towards me. 'Virgilio's precious Murano vase.' She grinned. 'Now that he's been promoted to *commissario*, it looks like he's joined the super-rich.'

As *commissario* is roughly the same rank as chief inspector, I felt I had to set the record straight. 'I'm afraid that police pay is a long way off those heights – in Italy or in England.'

She caught my eye. 'You don't need to tell me.' She gave a shrug of the shoulders, and I picked up on her words.

'Are you a police officer as well?' When Virgilio had told me he had a friend in Venice, I had wondered whether it might be somebody in the Venice force.

'I'm a detective inspector. I gather from Virgilio that you were a *commissario* at Scotland Yard. I've read enough detective stories to know how grand that place must be.'

I smiled back at her. 'I can think of many adjectives to apply to working at Scotland Yard, but I don't think "grand" would figure too highly. So, what's it like being a cop in Venice? London or Florence are bad enough with millions of visitors every year, but the sheer numbers coming into Venice must cause all sorts of problems for you.'

At that moment, the waiter returned with my beer and Giulia waited until he'd left again before replying. 'To be honest, when you consider how many tourists come here, they don't cause too much serious trouble. Most of them are sensible enough not to go around committing murders when they've got all this wonderful architecture to look at. No, most of my problems are related to the *malavita*.'

Malavita is a word the Italians use to describe the criminal underworld, particularly organised crime. Italy has quite a selection of home-grown criminal organisations ranging from the traditional Sicilian Mafia to some very unpleasant iterations such as the 'Ndrangheta or Camorra. Here in Venice, as Giulia went on to tell me, these were only the tip of the iceberg.

'As well as Italian criminals, we've seen increasing activity from gangs with connections to Albania, Slovakia and even China. When they aren't fighting each other, they squabble amongst themselves. You'd be amazed how often we have to pull bodies out of the canals.'

'And what are they fighting about? Are these turf wars for protection rackets, prostitution, drugs or what?'

'Drugs, mainly. As you can imagine, with so many vessels coming in and out every day, it's hard to keep a check on all of them. We work closely with the *Guardia di Finanza*, and they've had some spectacular successes recently. A few years ago, they managed to recover eight hundred and fifty kilos of cocaine hidden in the hull of a Greek vessel that arrived from Brazil. The estimated street value was a hundred and fifty million euros. You can see why the bad guys might fight to get hold of something like that.'

The *Guardia di Finanza* is a separate force in Italy, working in parallel with the *Polizia* and *Carabinieri*, principally concerned with financial matters, including smuggling. In our modern world of Internet fraud, I felt sure they had their hands full and, by the sound of it, here in Venice, smuggling was the name of the game.

Giulia and I chatted, and she sounded fascinated by my decision to open my own private investigation agency. She asked me if I was here on business or pleasure, and I told her I was taking part in a murder mystery weekend on the Island of the Swans. I didn't mention Alice Graceland by name, nor did I say that she was a film star. Giulia was clearly familiar with the island, but she hadn't realised – although she wasn't surprised – that the new owner was a foreigner. Virgilio had apparently told her about my books and she sounded intrigued. When I told her that my first book, *Death Amid the Vines*, had now come out in Italian, she promised to buy a copy and read it.

'One thing I regret is not having worked harder at English when I was at school.' She waved her hands vaguely in the direction of the crowds around us. 'There's no getting away from it, the international language of communication these days is English, and mine is decidedly broken. I'll certainly read your book now I know that it's available in Italian.'

I thoroughly enjoyed chatting to her but, all too soon, it was time for me to go and catch my lift back to the island. We shook hands and exchanged phone numbers before I picked up the precious parcel. 'I'll see that Virgilio gets this on Monday. Any time you're coming down to Florence, give me a call, and Virgilio and I will see that you get a good meal.'

9

FRIDAY AFTERNOON

When we got back to the island, I thanked Diego and went to my room with Oscar. When I got there, I dug his bowl out of my bag and gave him a long drink of cold water. I then turned my attention to a large paper parcel I saw lying on my bed. Sure enough, wrapped in brown paper was my costume for the murder mystery session tomorrow evening and for the dummy run tonight. I tipped the contents onto the bed and took stock.

It looked ominously similar to the costume I had had to wear on the set of the movie a couple of years back when I had met Selena Gardner and, more importantly, Anna. That movie, too, had been set in Renaissance times. I unfolded each of the articles and studied them. On top of the pile, there was a papier mâché mask that looked chilling. It wasn't a full face mask but more of a half-mask, covering the top half of the face. It was a sinister black with red around the eyeholes with a long, curved, beaky nose almost covering my mouth. I had a feeling it would be next to impossible to eat or drink while wearing something like this, but what lay below it was even worse. There was a white silk – or imitation silk – shirt, over which I would wear a deep-blue, velvet sleeveless gilet, trimmed with silver braid. That wasn't the problem, but my heart sank as I spotted the next article of clothing. It was a pair of baggy, blue and yellow pantaloons, composed of stripes of blue velvet and white silk. To make matters worse, there was a floppy hat, also made of blue velvet, with silver trimmings and a tassel at the back. I picked it up and spotted, nestling innocently underneath everything, what I'd been dreading most of all: a packet containing a pair of blue tights.

Oscar had finished his water by now and was sniffing the costume with interest. I don't know whether it stirred a distant memory in him, but he glanced up at me, and there was no mistaking the expression on his face. He was giving me a big, hairy, toothy, canine grin.

I didn't grin back.

'It's all right for you; nobody's making *you* dress up. I just hope all the activity takes place inside air-conditioned rooms, or at night. A combination of heavy velvet clothes, the silly hat and tights is going to make life pretty damn uncomfortable in this heat.'

Still, I told myself, I had no choice, so I would have to grin and bear it – or at least bear it while grinding my teeth. I checked the time and saw that it was already five o'clock, so that didn't leave me much time before the dress rehearsal. I took Oscar outside again and let him wander about, sniffing his surroundings, while I sat down on a stone bench and called Anna to check that she'd got safely to her friend's place in the Apennines and to give her a progress report. I felt quite jealous when she told me that she was up at fifteen hundred metres, where the temperature was a very pleasant twenty-one degrees. I told her that here in Venice it was at least 50 per cent hotter than that and when I related what I was going to have to wear tonight, I could hear her giggling.

'I'm beginning to wish I'd come with you now. I do love dressing up in Renaissance costume. But you've always enjoyed it as well, haven't you?'

What could I say? 'Yes, of course, it'll be fun.'

I caught Oscar's eye and read a fair shot of scepticism in it – and he wasn't the only one to feel that way.

By the time I'd struggled into my costume, I was already sweating, and the mask over my nose didn't help. When I went out of my room into the stifling heat of the Venetian summer evening, I could feel perspiration running down my back. It was, therefore, a considerable relief when I walked into the dining room to find that the air-con had been doing a fine job, and it was refreshingly cool in there. Oscar at my side kept casting suspicious looks in my direction. Although he appeared to have accepted that it really was me underneath the mask and the silly clothes, he was clearly unsettled.

As I walked in, I was greeted by Mary. I almost didn't recognise her at first, as she was dressed in a long, maroon, velvet dress trimmed with gold, and she had a simple, but elegant, black, lace mask around her eyes. She had bare shoulders, a pearl necklace, and her hair was tied back with a red and gold contraption, making her look like a painting I had once seen of Anne Boleyn. She gave me a smile and a little curtsy.

'My Lord Magistrate, good evening.' Her tone was formal and respectful.

I grinned as I saw Oscar stop and do a double take. What were these humans up to? Seeing his confusion, Mary reached down to fondle his ears, and he gradually started to look reassured.

Entering into the spirit of the evening, I swept off my silly hat and bowed towards her. 'Good evening, ma'am, and who might you be?'

'I'm the personal secretary to the Doge. My name is Maria.' She transferred her attention to Oscar, who was sniffing the hem of her dress with great interest. 'I see you've brought your faithful assistant. Come and let me introduce you to your fellow dinner guests, starting with the Doge himself.' She lowered her voice and changed to a less theatrical tone. 'Miss Graceland is playing the part of his wife, Donna Alicia, the lady who really runs the show in this version of Venetian history. She'll be here shortly.' I saw her check out my appearance. 'Valentina's done a great job on your costume. You really look the part of the Doge's chief enforcer.'

'That's what I'm supposed to be?'

'I hope so. Miss Graceland asked me to check out what the Doge's chief of police would have been called, and it's been tricky. The closest I could come up with was *Magistrato alla Milizia,* who was responsible for investigating "serious crimes". I reckon that'll do.'

She led me across the room towards where a man was seated on a throne-like chair, surrounded by a group of five other people, all decked out in convincing Renaissance costumes. Presumably, these were the actors Alice had mentioned. There were four men and two women, and I didn't need to be a Renaissance expert to see that the man at the centre of the group was dressed in the finest silks and lace, while two of the other men and both women were dressed in garments similar to my own – fine but not opulent – while the remaining man was wearing simpler clothes. One of the men had a red mask while the two women were adorned with elaborate, glittering masks trimmed with feathers.

Mary morphed back into her Renaissance character and made the introductions. She spoke in English and I could see that the actors understood. Of course, I told myself, as the guests tomorrow presumably wouldn't be likely to speak much Italian and, from what Mary had told me, Alice herself probably didn't speak more than a few words, fluency in English must have been a prerequisite. Mary started by addressing herself first to the Doge, the man in the middle.

'Your Excellency, ladies and gentlemen, this is Don Daniele, the Magistrate, the head of the Doge's police force, and a man to be feared and loathed in equal proportions.' I saw the man in simple clothes give a realistic shudder at the sound of my name, while the others didn't react – except for the Doge. He raised a regal hand in greeting towards me but made no comment while Mary pointed at Oscar and continued. 'With the Magistrate is his ferocious hound, trained to sniff out conspiracy wherever it may lie.'

Bang on cue, Oscar wandered over to the Doge and rather spoilt his 'ferocious hound' appellation by wagging his tail good-naturedly and licking the man's hand. Mary turned back and addressed me formally.

'My Lord Magistrate, of course you know the Doge well after working with him for years, but let me introduce you to the Doge's half-brother and his wife, along with Admiral Diodato, the head of the Venetian navy, a man of considerable substance.'

I checked them out and had to commend whoever had selected the actors for their roles. The Doge was smaller than I had expected, but he made up for any lack of height by emanating an aura of power. Giordano, the Doge's half-brother, was holding his mask in his hand, which meant that I was able to see his weaselly face, while his wife in her sumptuous, yellow, feathery mask positively exuded supercilious noblesse, even though I couldn't see her full face. As for the Admiral, he was certainly a man of substance. His wide leather belt barely retained his massive stomach, and the red mask across the top half of his face matched the colour of his cheeks, giving him the appearance of a freshly boiled beetroot. He looked as though he were about to explode at any minute.

Doing my best to enter into the spirit of the play, I bowed to the Doge and then adopted a haughty air, merely acknowledging the three nobles with the slightest nod of the head before transferring my attention to the remaining woman, who was wearing an unexpectedly revealing dark green and gold dress. 'And who is this young lady?'

Mary was on hand to introduce her. 'This is Donna Lucia, a courtesan, and the man behind her is Giorgio, the landlord of this inn.'

The landlord gave me a respectful bow, and Donna Lucia followed suit, although her neckline threatened a serious wardrobe malfunction as she leant forward. Her extravagant, feathery mask concealed her whole face, but when she clapped eyes on Oscar, she pushed it up onto the top of her head and gave him a broad smile.

'Hello, doggie. You're a looker, ain't you? Come and give us a kiss.' Her accent took me back to my life in London. She could have come straight from behind the bar of any number of East End pubs. I wondered idly what had brought her to Venice. Oscar, for his part, didn't bow but he trotted over, tail wagging, to say hello and found himself almost smothered by the warmth of her greeting.

Before I could initiate any kind of conversation, there was the sound of a door opening behind us and Alice Graceland appeared, dressed in a spectacular cream-coloured robe. She was wearing delicate, lace gloves to her elbows and her hair had been curled up onto her head and tied back with strings of pearls. She looked every bit the First Lady of Venice, and Oscar at my side obviously agreed as his tail started wagging furiously. She swept gracefully over and stopped to survey us with what looked like satisfaction.

'Excellent. You all look the part.' She, too, was speaking English. She turned to Mary. 'Mary, I think Oscar could do with a bow around his neck. Could you organise that for tomorrow, please?' Without waiting for an answer, she turned back towards our group. 'Thank you all for coming. For any of you unfamiliar with murder mysteries, I'll just run through the basics of what's going to happen. I would like you to all be back here on the island by six tomorrow at the latest. That should give you ample time to get changed and ready. The guests will assemble, either here or outside under the pergola, at or after six o'clock, and you then join them at seven. It will be your job to move around among them, giving them all a chance to speak to you. As you do so, I want you to pass on a few clues that may help them when trying to establish the identity of the murderer. I'll let you have these clues later this evening. Each of the guests will have received a card with a brief background to their character. Obviously, they will be all be instructed not to reveal what's on their cards to anybody.'

The Admiral raised a hand. 'Excuse me, but could I ask a question, please?' To my surprise, he had a strong Yorkshire accent. 'Who's going to get murdered? Is it going to be one of us?'

Alice shook her head. 'The victim will be me.' This came as another surprise to me, but Alice went on to explain. 'I play the part of the real ruler of the Venetian Republic, the power behind the throne. The Doge himself is completely in my thrall and, as a result, I have collected a considerable number of enemies, jealous of my power. All of the guests will be given cards explaining who they are and why every single one of them would dearly like to see me dead. Just to complicate things for them when they try to work out who did it, all of you will also have reasons for wanting me, Donna Alicia, the Doge's wife, to die.'

I caught her eye. 'I gather that I'm the Magistrate. Does this mean that I'm impartial?'

'Indeed. You are the investigating officer. It'll be up to you to draw all the different strands together and, at the end of the evening, to give each of the guests the opportunity to point the finger at the person they believe to be responsible for the murder. Once everybody has said their piece, you will reveal the identity of the murderer and reward whoever has got it right.' She looked around at all of us. 'The basic premise of the story is that we have escaped from an outbreak of plague in the city and are hunkered down here in this isolated inn until the disease passes and it's safe to return to Venice again. Is that clear to all of you?'

The Cockney courtesan had a question. 'What happens to you, Donna Alicia, after the murder? Do you just lie on the ground with a dagger in your heart or a rope around your neck, or do you continue to play a part even after your supposed death?'

Alice nodded. 'The murder will take place right at the end of the meal, so I shouldn't have to wait too long for the denouement. I'll just pretend to be dead and listen in to the conversation until everything is revealed. The important thing is for you all to circulate among the guests in the course of the evening and to pass on the clues that I'll give you. Please keep these to yourself until tomorrow as this will enhance the experience if nobody knows in advance who the murderer is. Is that clear?'

There were murmurs of agreement, and she continued.

'I'm delighted you've all brought masks, and this will further confuse the guests in their investigations.' She produced a golden mask from behind her back and put it on. This was a full face mask with a blank, pitiless expression that looked downright scary. The top half of the mask with the eyeholes was solid, while the lower half over her mouth was made of golden lace, concealing her lips but presumably allowing her to eat and drink without having to remove it. 'Thank you in advance for your efforts. Now, I suggest that you all help yourselves to a drink and get to know each other, but please do try to stay in character. Dinner will be served in an hour, so that should hopefully give you time to talk among yourselves and refine your backstories.'

She waved towards a side table where Diego and his son, both wearing leather trousers, aprons and floppy hats, were standing by with bottles and glasses. I was delighted to see that Alice's desire for Renaissance authenticity hadn't extended to the drinks – at least for tonight – and I headed across to grab a bottle of cold Beck's beer. As I did so, I pulled my mask up onto the top of my head and gave Diego a wink.

'So how come you two get to wear trousers, and I have to wear these damn tights?'

He glanced down at my legs and grinned. 'Me, I'm only a servant. You're a noble, and nobles wear tights. Uncomfortable?'

In response, I just grimaced. Before beginning to circulate among the other actors, I studied Alice's face for a few moments. She had removed the golden mask again and she looked animated. I walked over and asked a question that had been playing on my mind.

'I'm impressed by your murder mystery story, Alice... sorry, Donna Alicia. Are you going to give me the name of the murderer in advance, or am I expected to work it out for myself?'

'Normally, in these circumstances, the person playing the part of the detective is given the answer in advance, but I've been wondering whether maybe, out of professional pride, you might like to pit your wits against me. It's your call completely.'

I stood there and gave it some thought. The obvious, sensible answer was to ask her to furnish me with the name of the murderer in advance, but I was in two minds. Once a detective, always a detective – maybe I should take her on. In the end, I came up with a compromise. 'I must admit that it would be fun to try to work it out for myself, but I'm conscious that your murder mystery evening needs an impressive ending, so why don't we do this? You don't tell me who did it, but you give me a sealed envelope with the killer's name in it. That way, if you completely bamboozle me, I can open the envelope, and the evening can still go off with a bang.'

She gave an approving nod. 'An excellent suggestion. I'll give you the envelope at start of play tomorrow evening.'

10

SATURDAY MORNING

I was up early on Saturday to give Oscar a walk. I had checked with Diego the previous night and he had suggested taking Oscar across to the Lido where there was a lot more space. As I left my room, I spotted Diego in the garden and went over to get the key to the outboard motor of the little boat. He led me down the ramp to the jetty and showed me how to work the engine. It was reassuringly similar to one I had used before, so I felt reasonably confident – as long as I didn't get run over by a ferry or a cruise liner. Diego told me where I could moor up but warned me to make sure I didn't stray from the specific place he mentioned, for fear of getting a parking fine. Venice really was just like any other city, give or take a bit of water.

Oscar jumped willingly into the boat and would probably have carried on over the other side and into the water if I hadn't been hanging onto his lead. I waved an admonitory finger at him and looped the end of his lead around my ankle when I sat down. I knew of old how difficult it was to drag fifty or sixty pounds of soggy canine bone and muscle out of the water and into a boat, and I wanted to avoid that at all costs.

The trip across to the Lido was remarkably straightforward and took less than ten minutes. Diego's directions had been spot on, and I easily managed to find the parking area he had indicated. I manoeuvred the boat to a mooring by the shore, and Oscar and I set off to explore.

The first thing I discovered came as something of a shock to the system. Everywhere I looked, there were roads, and line upon line of parked cars. A quick look at a conveniently situated map of the Lido showed me that this wasn't an island but a long, slim breakwater, barely a couple of hundred metres wide, dividing the lagoon from the open sea, and it was connected to the mainland at the northern end. As a result, almost every available space had been built on and along with the houses and the people had inevitably come the cars. I kept Oscar on the lead just to be on the safe side, although at seven in the morning, there wasn't much traffic. It was remarkable how different the atmosphere was compared to the old city across the water. Here, I found myself among apartment blocks and hotels, by the look of them, most built in the twentieth century. The main roads themselves were pleasantly wide and lined with trees, but there wasn't much in the way of open space for Oscar to run around. Still, I made sure we both did a decent circuit before I spotted a café already open where I sat down for a coffee and a brioche. As always, Oscar disposed of the tail end of my bun.

While I sat there, I thought back to the dress rehearsal the previous night. It had gone remarkably smoothly. Dinner had been served out on the terrace and had started with a combination of drinks and canapés, allowing the actors to wander around, mingling with the non-existent guests and chatting among themselves in readiness for the main event today. Although it hadn't been easy, I had gradually managed to get the hang of eating and drinking with my mask on, in spite of my massive hooked nose.

During the sit-down meal, after every course, we'd had to get up and change seats so as to allow us all to communicate with each other. I had a feeling there might be a certain amount of resistance from the guests at tonight's main event, particularly some of the more elderly ones – and they made up the majority – but I hadn't said anything.

I'd seen that the actors had all been issued with cards containing clues for them to pass on to the guests. As far as I could see, they had obeyed Alice's instructions not to discuss these with the others, although I'd seen our host take each of them aside for a one-to-one briefing in the course of the evening. I was most impressed at the time and effort Alice must have put into planning the event, and I had a feeling that her guests were going to be similarly impressed.

After my cup of coffee, I headed back to the island and when I got there, I found Mary waiting for me on the jetty.

'Hi, Dan, Diego told me you'd gone over to the Lido in the dinghy, and I spotted you coming back. I thought I'd let you have the accommodation list, so you know who's in which room.' She handed me a sheet of paper and a little paper bag with one hand while fending off a warm greeting from Oscar with the other. 'And here's a bow to tie to Oscar's collar tonight. Miss Graceland wants him to look good. I'm just waiting for Diego now. We've got a busy morning ahead of us. We've had arrival details from the guests and we're going over to the airport now to collect Jack Sloane, Maggie McBride and her boyfriend, along with Alastair Groves and his wife.' She glanced at her watch. 'They're arriving pretty soon from Rome and then, once we've dropped them off here, we'll be going straight back to the airport again to pick up the two actors, Dirk Foster and Lucy O'Connell, along with Desmond Norman – they're flying in on Norman's private jet. If they're on time, we should be able to drop them off here before zooming back to the airport one more time to pick up Greg Gupta and Carlos Rodriguez, who're coming in on the morning flight from Berlin.'

I did a bit of mental arithmetic. 'What about Wilfred Baker and his companion?'

She shook her head. 'No word yet how they're getting to Venice, but he's told Miss Graceland he's going to make his own way out to the island – presumably by water taxi.'

While we were chatting, Diego came hurrying down the ramp and jumped into the launch. As he passed me, I gave him back the keys to the dinghy and left them to it.

When I got back to my room, first things first, I gave Oscar his breakfast and then I opened the paper bag and pulled out an intricate bow made of wide, red ribbon. A couple of strings hanging from it would be used to tie it to his collar. As long as he didn't eat it – he has an inexhaustible and fairly indiscriminate appetite – I felt sure he would look suitably impressive. I put it with my magistrate's costume and settled down to catch up on paperwork Lina had sent me from Florence.

At just before ten, there was a tap on my door, and I opened it to find Alice Graceland herself standing there. She was wearing shorts and a baggy T-shirt, but she still looked amazing.

'Good morning, Alice.' It still felt strange to be calling such a huge star by her first name.

'Good morning, Dan. I've brought you some more information about what's going to happen tonight. Feel like a walk?'

This resulted in an immediate reaction from Oscar, who slipped out through Alice's legs into the garden. I followed – not through Alice's legs – and the two of us walked slowly around for a couple of minutes, just chatting, until we came level with the greenhouse. I pointed towards the mass of vegetation in there and pulled out my phone.

'I'm most impressed with what you've done to the gardens, and I don't think I've ever seen a greenhouse with so many plants in it. I don't recognise half of them, and I wonder if you'd mind if I took a look inside some time. I've got an app on my phone that claims to be able to recognise virtually every plant on the planet, and I'd like to put it to the test.'

Her response was enthusiastic. 'I would be fascinated. Like you, I haven't been able to recognise many of the plants either and I hadn't thought about getting an app. Before I bought the island, somebody was using the place as a market garden – illegally, as it belonged to the city and was off limits – growing fruit and vegetables. I've no idea what nationality they were, but I have a feeling they weren't Italian. Apart from some familiar vegetables, there were also all sorts of exotic ones like mangoes and even papaya, and goodness only knows what's inside the greenhouse.' She glanced at her watch. 'I wish I could spare the time to accompany you now, but I'm going to need to go back to change pretty soon, before the first of the guests arrive. If you do feel like taking a look around in the greenhouse, I'd be very grateful if you could let me know what you find.'

I agreed immediately, and we carried on walking until we reached one of the stone staircases leading to the ramparts and climbed it. We went across to one of the larger openings in the outside wall, from where we could look back across the lagoon towards the city to the left, and further over the islands of Murano and Burano to the right. As I looked on, there was a distant roar and I saw an aircraft coming in to land at Venice's Marco Polo airport – maybe carrying some of tonight's guests. Alice stood beside me and talked me through what would happen this evening, until I had a pretty good idea. She ended by shooting me a decidedly cheeky wink.

'If all goes as I've planned it, there's going to be a twist in the tail right at the end. Hopefully, it'll surprise the guests and, who knows, maybe even bamboozle the experienced detective.'

I smiled back at her. 'I've always liked a challenge. I'm sure it's all going to go really well. But don't forget to give me the sealed envelope with the identity of the murderer just in case you really do bamboozle me.'

She gave a gleeful chuckle. 'I promise I won't forget the envelope. And please come and join me and the other guests at lunchtime. Valentina's going to serve drinks on the terrace from midday. I'll introduce you to everybody.'

Then she gave Oscar a final tummy rub – he had been lying stretched out at her feet – and set off back down the steps again. I stood there admiring the view for another minute or two and then headed for the greenhouse.

It was so overgrown in there that I told Oscar to stay outside just in case there were slug pellets or other poisonous things lying around, and I squeezed my way in between what my phone identified as a persimmon tree, *Diospyros kaki*, and a fortunately abandoned wasps' nest the size of a basketball. Above my head was a vine, hung with the most amazing blue flowers with unusual, prominent, yellow stamens, and dotted among the flowers were strange orange and purple fruits, the size of large apricots. The phone identified this as *Passiflora edulis* or passion fruit. I carried on down the length of the greenhouse, feeling like a Victorian explorer in the jungle, gradually collecting plant names ranging from *Litchi chinensis* and *Cerbera odollam* to *Psidium guajava*. By the time I emerged again, I had a list of half a dozen Latin plant names that meant nothing to me whatsoever, and I resolved to do my best to find English names for everything when I had time, so I could pass the list on to Alice.

Back in my room, before plunging once more into a complicated quotation for a racing stables on the outskirts of Florence who believed their horses were being nobbled by rival racehorse owners or betting cheats, I went through in my head what Alice had told me. I was to meet up with the new arrivals on the terrace before lunch for drinks. She knew her guests well and had told me that this might turn out to be an alcoholic event for some of them, after which, a few would probably retire to their rooms for a siesta, while others might prefer to laze by the pool, or even take a trip into Venice to see the sights.

At the end of the afternoon, changed into our costumes, we would all meet up again on the terrace at six, and the murder mystery evening would begin. From the way Alice had described it, the drinks would be followed by the evening meal on the terrace, like last night, involving musical chairs between courses. This would probably take a couple of hours, during which the guests and actors would mingle and exchange information until the murder took place. When Alice lay apparently dead, it would be my job to collect everybody together and give them all a chance to voice their suspicions until the killer could be revealed.

By my calculations, this probably meant that the murder mystery part of the evening would be done and dusted by nine or nine-thirty. This struck me as pretty early for a party to finish until it occurred to me that a number of the guests were well over seventy, so maybe nine-thirty was bedtime for some, if not all. At least this would mean that Oscar got his evening walk at a reasonable hour.

And it would mean I could remove the dreaded tights before they cut off my circulation completely.

11

SATURDAY LUNCHTIME

Oscar and I walked across to the terrace at noon. Fortunately it was a bit less oppressively hot today, with a hint of a breeze rustling the leaves in the pergola above my head. I found Diego serving glasses of sparkling wine to a little group of four or five people. As I approached, I did my best to associate the photos I'd seen on the Internet with the people before me.

Dirk Foster was the easiest to identify. I knew the veteran actor to be seven years older than me, but I didn't need a mirror to know that he looked far, far younger. He was tall, probably a couple of inches taller than me, his perfectly hydrated skin glowed with an even, golden tan, and his immaculately styled hair didn't have a single speck of grey in it. Alongside him was a figure that I didn't recognise immediately. I had to give her a second or a third glance before I realised that the rather frumpy woman alongside him with a scruffy mop of short, unkempt hair – quite possibly cut by herself – was none other than Lucy O'Connell. Considering that the Internet had told me that she was only forty-two and she'd been voted the sexiest woman in the world only a few years earlier, her deterioration was startling.

Just behind them was a white-haired old man slumped on a seat, smoking the biggest cigar I'd ever seen in my life. I might be exaggerating slightly, but it looked almost the size of a rolling pin. I've never smoked, but I had to admit that it did smell good. He was easily recognisable as Desmond Norman, the legendary movie mogul, and to his left was another elderly man, this time a considerably fatter man, who was wiping copious amounts of sweat off his face with a handkerchief the size of a small towel. This had to be Jack Sloane, the casting director with an eye for outstanding talent, whose phone number had achieved legendary status.

As I approached them from one side, a couple approached from the other, and I couldn't miss Maggie McBride, widow of Caspar McBride the oil billionaire, allegedly one of the richest women on the planet. From where I was standing, she looked far younger than her sixty-two years, while the slim, swarthy man half her age on her arm fell neatly into the 'Latin lover' category that Alice had described, even down to the shirt open almost to his navel and a gold medallion the size of a chocolate Hobnob on his hairy chest. I didn't bother checking him for tattoos, or to see how tight his trousers were. I decided I would take Alice's word for that.

I was just in the process of helping myself to a glass of fizz – no beer on offer – when a shrill whistle split the air and both Oscar and I turned around to see Alice herself with two fingers at her lips, calling Oscar. She crouched down, opened her arms, and he didn't need to be asked twice. He shot across the paving slabs to bury himself in her arms, tail wagging furiously.

'That's a handsome dog you have there.'

I turned back to find myself being addressed by none other than Dirk Foster, multi-Oscar-winning star of more blockbuster movies than I could shake a stick at. I did my best to look as if chatting to global megastars was an everyday occurrence for me.

'Thanks for the compliment. As I expect you'll find out, Oscar has very good taste when it comes to women. I'm thinking of hiring him out to judge beauty pageants.' I held out my hand towards the great man. 'I'm Dan. I'm going to be the detective in tonight's little play.'

He gave me a charming smile that showed off some very expensive dental work, while I did my best not to yelp with pain as he shook my hand. He didn't bother introducing himself. Very few people on the planet were unfamiliar with his face. 'So how do you know the lovely Alice?'

From the way he said it, I got the feeling he maybe wasn't as fond of her as might have been expected. I told him briefly about our shared friendship with Selena Gardner and I got the impression that Selena wasn't high in his book of favourite actors either. Maybe he just hated everybody.

At that moment, we were descended upon by Maggie McBride – and I use that expression advisedly. She suddenly materialised alongside Foster, relinquished her hold on her Latin lover, and threw her arms around Foster's neck – or at least she tried to. Seen close up, she was far smaller than I had imagined, in spite of wearing a pair of high heels that made it look as though she were on tiptoe. He bent forward obligingly and allowed her to deposit two smacking kisses on his cheeks, but I couldn't miss his expression of resignation as she assaulted him.

'Dirk, darling, the older you get, the more desirable you become.' Even I couldn't miss the exaggerated Southern belle accent. I glanced at her boyfriend, who was standing back obediently with a fixed smile on his handsome features. It occurred to me that – just like Labradors in hot weather – the life of a toyboy wasn't always a bundle of fun.

Foster stepped back and produced another gleaming smile that looked almost sincere – but he was a very good actor, after all.

'Maggie, my dear. How lovely to see you again.' I wasn't convinced that he meant it.

'I'm sure it is.' Maggie McBride's tone was at odds with her smile. In spite of the outward show of affection, I had a feeling there was no love lost between these two.

'You look stunning, as always.' I was sure that even Oscar could hear the lack of sincerity in his voice.

Maggie McBride made no comment, and I wasn't prepared for what happened next. She turned and, before I could take evasive action, grabbed me by the shoulders, pulled me down towards her and slapped a couple of kisses on my cheeks as well. 'Well, hi there, handsome. How come I haven't seen you around before?'

I stepped back in my turn and searched for a satisfactory response. 'I'm not in the movie business; I'm a detective.' Maybe I was still in a state of shock after her effusive greeting, but for a split second, I saw what might have been a shadow run across her face before she plastered on another smile.

'A detective! How exciting. And what are you detecting here? Maybe you think I've been a naughty, naughty girl.' She held out her wrists towards me. 'Clap on the handcuffs and I'll come quietly.' She then burst into a peal of raucous laughter and shot a lascivious glance at her boyfriend. 'Quiet's not my style though, is it, honey?'

I was relieved to feel a friendly nudge down at knee level and then a tap on my shoulder. I glanced around and saw Oscar and Alice beside me. I ruffled his ears and gave her a smile that probably came across as a cry for help, because she immediately stepped forward and encircled Maggie McBride in an exaggerated hug that might or might not have been genuine. 'Maggie, darling, you really are incorrigible. Leave these lovely men alone.' When she stepped back, I definitely got the impression that she was struggling to maintain the appearance of a warm welcome towards the other woman. 'You haven't introduced me to your significant other.' She turned towards the Latin lover. 'You must be the handsome Italian I've been hearing about.'

He stepped forward and held out his hand. 'My name is Rocco.' He had a strong Italian accent. 'All my life, I've wanted to meet you, Signora Graceland. I've seen every film you've ever been in and I think you're wonderful.' He sounded as though he meant it, and for a moment, I saw Maggie's lips tighten. Presumably, toyboy compliments were to be reserved for the partner of the hour.

Alice gave him a big smile, shook his hand and then glanced back at Maggie. 'Now tell me straight, Maggie: did you train him to say that?'

Maggie McBride shook her head. 'No, he did it all by himself.' She could have been talking about a prize poodle that had just learned to stand on its hind legs. 'He has a thing about beautiful women.'

I distinctly saw Dirk Foster roll his eyes, before he politely excused himself and headed off in the direction of the two elderly men. I decided to follow his example, shot both women a smile, and turned away, just in time to almost bump into a couple who had emerged from a nearby room. I recognised them as Carlos Rodriguez, the famous director, and Greg Gupta, scriptwriter par excellence. I held up an apologetic hand.

'Sorry to bump into you, gentlemen. I'm Dan.'

Rodriguez produced a conspiratorial grin. 'No problem. Greg and I saw you making a break for freedom. Maggie can have that effect on the unwary.' His accent was pure California.

Gupta grinned as well. 'They don't call her the man-eater for nothing.' He held out his hand toward me. 'Hi, I'm Greg, and this is Carlos.'

We all shook hands as Oscar finally managed to tear himself away from Alice and wandered over to say hello while I explained what I was doing here. To my surprise, Gupta already knew more about me than I had expected.

'Selena was talking about you just the other day.' He turned to Rodriguez. 'This guy's a dynamite private eye, and Selena told me he saved her life. Would you believe that?'

I was then forced to give them a brief summary of how I had met Selena Gardner, but I had to admit that I hadn't actually stepped into the line of fire to save her life. 'Yes, I helped the Florence police to catch the killer, but there's only one hero around here and that's Oscar.' I pointed down and he wagged his tail proudly. This wasn't news to him.

We stood and chatted, mainly about murder mystery parties – they had a lot more experience of them than I did – before I nudged the conversation on to the other guests. 'Do you guys know Dirk Foster well? I may be wrong, but I got the feeling he maybe doesn't really want to be here.'

The two men eyed each other before Gupta replied. 'To be honest, we were surprised to see him here as well.' He lowered his voice and leant towards me. 'Maybe you don't know that he and Alice had a thing together back in the mists of time, or do you?'

This was certainly news to me, so I shook my head and he elaborated. 'We're talking twenty years ago or more. It was one of those whirlwind Hollywood romances back in the days before everything was all over social media, and the studio did a pretty good job of hushing it up. Alice and Dirk were playing opposite each other in a romcom called *Santiago or Bust*.' He and

Rodriguez exchanged glances again before both adopted the same facial expression of distaste. 'Let's be charitable and just say it wasn't the best movie ever made.'

Rodriguez caught my eye and winked. 'On a scale of one to ten, we're talking about minus five.'

I found it fascinating that Alice had chosen to invite her former boyfriend. Was this with a view to rekindling that romance? If so, the fact that he wasn't looking too happy to be here made me think that maybe he didn't feel the same way. I was just going to ask for more detail when Gupta obligingly provided it.

'Nobody knows for sure, but they say the romance only lasted a matter of months, maybe even just weeks. What's sure is that when it broke down, it came complete with more insults and recrimination – on both sides – than the average catfight. Alice disappeared off the scene for a full year afterwards. There were voices saying that she'd gone to a spiritual retreat in India, and others swearing blind they'd seen her working in a leper colony in Africa. Wherever it was that she went, when she finally reappeared, she refused to talk to Dirk or even acknowledge his existence, and they've never worked together since. The word on the street is that Desmond Norman's studios have offered them an astronomical sum if they agree to star in a movie together but, so far, no joy. They've still been keeping their distance. That's why we were so surprised to see him here.' He suddenly switched topic to the beauties of Venice and out of the corner of my eye, I saw Alice approaching.

'Hi, guys, I'm so glad you could come.' She gave them a smile that looked pretty sincere, but I wasn't totally convinced. Did she have a problem with these men as well? Gupta answered for both of them while Rodriguez looked decidedly uncomfortable.

'Hi, Alice, long time no see. We were just saying a few months ago how it was time we came back to Venice and did the city properly. We were here two years ago for the film festival, but neither of us got much time off. We're booked into the Danieli from Monday for the rest of next week and we plan on seeing everything that needs seeing.'

'What do you think of my new best friend?' For a moment, I thought Alice might be referring to me but then saw the direction in which her hand was pointing. 'Isn't he gorgeous? I keep meaning to get myself another dog since Mimi died and I've been putting it off for too long.' She reached down and stroked Oscar's head affectionately before glancing up at me. 'I don't suppose you'd feel like leaving him with me, would you, Dan?'

I shook my head. 'Sorry, Alice, but where I go, he goes. We're joined at the hip.'

Another couple emerged from their room and as they came along the terrace towards us, I sensed an increase in tension in our hostess. The two newcomers were a distinguished-looking grey-haired gentleman, who looked to be in his seventies. He was leaning heavily on a walking stick, and at his side was a woman probably around the same age, with unnaturally blonde hair, and she looked far less frail than her husband. This had to be Alastair Groves, Alice's former agent, and his wife, Sandra, although the photo I had seen of him online had shown him as far more fit and mobile. I wondered what had happened. Clearly, Alice already knew.

'Alastair, how're you feeling? Was the flight terribly uncomfortable?' She threw a couple of air kisses at him before doing the same to his wife. In spite of her expression of concern for his health and the kisses – none of which came anywhere near hitting the mark – I got the distinct feeling that her greeting towards both was forced, and Mrs Groves, in particular, looked far from thrilled to be here. Once again, I couldn't help wondering why on earth Alice had thought of inviting people to her party that she didn't like – and why they had accepted her invitation. Something didn't add up.

Groves sounded weary when he answered. 'Alice, hi. Today was a short flight up from Rome, so it was okay. The worst was when we came over from the States earlier in the week, and I had to do the whole flight lying flat.' I wondered what had happened to him. Maybe a hip transplant or something like that?

Alice still had her welcoming smile on her face – but even though she was a very good actress, I sensed that it was wearing thin. Nevertheless, she still managed to sound solicitous when she replied.

'I'm so sorry to hear that. Hopefully, you'll be comfortable here. At least there aren't any cars here on the island. Did the cops manage to catch the driver who did this to you?' As he shook his head, she glanced at me and explained. 'Alastair was involved in a hit and run. He's lucky to be alive.'

That answered that. During my online research, I hadn't seen any mention of this, but I had discovered that Alastair Groves was one of the top three agents in Hollywood, with a string of A-listers on his books, and I found myself wondering why Alice had severed relations with him. I'd been able to find very little information about his wife, except for the fact that they had apparently met at university and had now been married for over fifty years – a rarity in Hollywood.

Alice stepped back after greeting them, and there was an awkward silence for a few moments before, by tacit agreement, the new arrivals turned and went off. Alice waited until they were out of earshot before murmuring in my ear. 'The car accident couldn't have happened to a more deserving person.' And then she wafted off to talk to some of the others.

I looked down at Oscar, who was watching her leave with a wistful expression on his face, the end of his tail wagging slowly, and it occurred to me that he was probably one of the few guests genuinely happy to be here.

Not the ideal ingredients for a cosy house party.

12

SATURDAY AFTERNOON

Lunch was announced by three strikes of a magnificent brass gong and served in the dining room. We all sat around the long table with Alice at the head, flanked by Desmond Norman and Maggie McBride. Oscar and I took up position down at the far end, where I found myself with Jack Sloane, the casting director, on my right and two empty seats to my left. Sloane dropped his considerable bulk into his seat with a grunt, and I distinctly heard the fine antique mahogany chair groan in protest. He retrieved yet another voluminous handkerchief from his sleeve and wiped his forehead.

'Finally, some air-con. God, it's hot out there.' He appeared to be addressing the empty seats opposite him, but I replied all the same.

'I'm afraid Venice has a reputation for being hot in summer and freezing cold in winter.'

He glanced sideways at me. 'Then why the hell didn't Alice have her party in winter?' He transferred his gaze to Oscar, who was sitting to attention alongside me, adopting his 'faithful but starving' look. His nose had already told him that there were breadsticks on the table. 'This your dog? You blind or something?'

As a conversation starter, it wouldn't have won any prizes for tact, but I'd met enough rude characters in my time. 'He's a sniffer dog. I hope you haven't got any drugs in your pocket.'

He shook his head irritably. 'Drugs? Why the hell would I want drugs? I never felt the need.' He wiped another wave of sweat off his forehead. 'But that's all they think of these days.' He lowered his voice – a fraction – and shot a glance up the table towards where Lucy O'Connell was sitting, hopefully out of earshot. 'I've seen enough of what drugs do to folk. Check out Lucy. When I first met her, I thought she was the most beautiful woman in the world, but just look at her now. Drugs! What's wrong with people?'

I was saved from having to reply to this deep philosophical conundrum by the arrival of the last two guests. It was easy to work out that these had to be Wilfred Baker and his girlfriend, Antoinette.

Alice greeted them with a wave.

'Hi, Freddie, we were getting worried!' She didn't look particularly worried, and I noted that she didn't include his partner in her greeting. 'Come here and give me a kiss.'

I took a closer look at the famous film director as he headed for our host. I remembered reading that he was forty-three but if I hadn't known, I don't think I would have guessed. He wasn't a tall man and he was wearing the clumsiest pair of trainers I'd ever seen in my life. Presumably, these golden monstrosities with unbelievably thick soles were the latest thing in the world of fashion, with the added advantage of giving him an extra couple of inches of height. Above these were skinny white jeans that finished mid-calf, and a blue and white striped shirt that gave him a vaguely nautical look. From the neck downwards, he could have been in his twenties. From the neck upwards, he could have been in his sixties. He had a straggly little Fu Manchu beard that was turning grey, and the rest of his face and the whole of his head had been shaved clean.

His girlfriend stayed down at my end of the table while he went up to greet Alice. I found myself wondering whether her decision not to go with him had been her own choice or whether she, like Maggie McBride's toyboy, Rocco, knew her place and automatically occupied a secondary role. She caught my eye and I gave her a smile, but the hint of a smile she gave me in return was one of resignation. Somehow, I got the impression that being the guest of a world-famous film star on a gorgeous island in the historic Venetian lagoon didn't appeal to her as much as I might have expected. Either that, or she wasn't enjoying the company of her gold-shoe-clad boyfriend.

When it came to choosing the guests for her party, Alice appeared to have got things drastically wrong – or had she? Could it be that she had deliberately invited people who didn't like her and, if so, why? Presumably, if they didn't like her, she didn't like them, so why should she have chosen to invite people she didn't like? I glanced down at Oscar, who was still sitting to attention, trying to look as if he were in the latter stages of starvation, and reflected once again that, apart from him, hardly anybody around the table looked happy to be here. This really didn't seem like the recipe for a happy weekend get-together.

Freddie leant towards Alice and the two of them air-kissed theatrically, missing each other by miles. I wasn't close enough to be able to analyse their facial expressions, but there was something about the body language of both of them that told me that this apparently friendly reunion was anything but. When he and his girlfriend took their seats close to where I was, I gave him a welcoming smile but got nothing in return. He remained stony-faced and didn't say a word – not even to his companion. Clearly, this was somebody else for whom this weekend didn't look like being a bundle of laughs.

Lunch was excellent. Valentina and Gabriella moved around the table serving a selection of antipasti ranging from at least six different types of salami, homemade Russian salad and sliced tomatoes with basil and mozzarella, to mussels au gratin and fried soft-shell crabs. Diego followed on his wife's heels offering a choice of an excellent Chardonnay from the north of the Veneto region, or a fifteen-year-old Barolo from Piedmont. I opted for a glass of the Chardonnay and made it last. I had no intention of getting plastered at lunchtime. Jack Sloane to my right, on the other hand, clearly thought differently and surprised Diego by asking for a glass of white *and* a glass of red so he could 'try them'. By the time Diego had gone around the table once, Sloane had made up his mind – after emptying both glasses. He gave Diego a peremptory wave and delivered his verdict.

'I'll drink the red. You can leave the bottle.'

On the other side of me was Freddie Baker's girlfriend, Antoinette Latour, and I introduced myself to her. Although Baker completely ignored me, she at least was prepared to talk. She told me – in excellent English – that they had driven here from Milan, and Freddie had rented a speedboat to get to the island – even though the local speed limit had restricted them to near walking speed. She told me that she was originally from Nice, so we chatted a little about the Riviera coast. I knew it from the Italian side, and it was interesting to hear just how similar the geography, customs and even traditional dishes were on either side of the border. Freddie Baker continued to say nothing to anybody, and I noticed that he didn't touch either the fish or the wine, making do with just some breadsticks, a few slices of tomato, and a glass of mineral water. Antoinette, on the other hand, tried all the different antipasti and accompanied them with a glass of Chardonnay.

I was fascinated – and somewhat taken aback – to see Jack Sloane get through the whole bottle of red in the course of his antipasti alone. Diego proved to be not only good at driving the launch, but also an attentive wine waiter and he had been watching. He materialised barely a minute later to open another bottle, replenish Sloane's glass, and set the bottle down in front of him. Understandably, Sloane had been too occupied eating and drinking to do much talking, and it was only after the antipasti plates had been cleared away that he shot a few words across the table towards Freddie Baker – but it wasn't light table talk.

'What you working on now?' He produced his napkin and gave his face and forehead another wipe. 'Hopefully, something a damn sight better than that awful musical. Whatever possessed you to turn your hand to a musical, for God's sake?'

I looked across at Freddie with interest, wondering how he was going to respond, but, to my surprise, he just laughed – at first. '*Dancing and Singing* has grossed half a billion dollars in less than a year. Maybe it wasn't so awful after all.' His expression became more hostile. 'I've heard people saying that you've lost your edge, Jack; you're getting too old. I didn't want to believe them, but maybe they were right after all. You've lost it. You can't tell a blockbuster from a lame duck.'

I saw another couple of faces turn towards Freddie, and there was a sudden silence at our end of the table. Sloane dropped his napkin back onto his lap and gave Freddie a belligerent glare. 'Beginner's luck can't compete with half a century of picking winners, Freddie. Your luck will change before long, while I'll still be riding high.'

His right hand reached out for his wine glass and, for a moment, I wondered if he was going to throw the contents across the table at the younger man but, instead, he raised it to his mouth and drained it. 'I've seen countless pretty boys like you come and go. You wait, before long, you'll be going round knocking on doors, begging for work.'

I felt a movement at my feet and saw Oscar looking up at me with a quizzical expression on his face. I don't want to give the impression that he understands everything he hears, but he certainly registers mood remarkably accurately. I reached down and scratched his ears as I did my best to defuse what was turning into a volatile situation at this end of the table by changing the subject – slightly. I addressed myself to Freddie Baker.

'Have you ever worked with Alice Graceland, Mr Baker?'

He carried on glaring at Sloane for a few more seconds before turning towards me. 'No, I've never had that pleasure.' His reply was terse, and I felt that his choice of vocabulary was deliberately insincere.

Before I could reply, Sloane stepped in. 'Alice would never work with you, Freddie, and even if she wanted to, Louie would never allow it.'

Still trying to turn this into a normal conversation, I queried the name. 'I'm sorry, Louie? Who's Louie?'

Freddie Baker answered without taking his eyes off Sloane for a second. 'Jack's referring to Alice's agent, Louis Leder. He's another old man like Jack, soon to be on the junk heap like Jack.'

There was a sinister growl from the big man, possibly presaging a volcanic eruption, and it came as a welcome distraction at that moment to see Valentina arrive at our shoulders with a huge steaming dish of risotto. Silence fell once more as she served the rice and we all started eating. I've never been a great fan of rice – unless it's buried beneath a liberal helping of curry – but this was excellent. I could taste mushrooms and maybe smoked ham, with more than a hint of truffles, and it was predictably delicious. As I ate, I reflected on the tetchy exchange between the two men, and this confirmed the feeling I had already begun to get that at least some of the guests not only were not that keen on our host, but were also not that keen on each other.

* * *

After an afternoon spent finishing off some work that Lina had sent me, I finally closed my laptop at five and took Oscar out for a little walk around the garden. I heard splashing and wandered over to the pool in the centre to find two people in the water. They couldn't have been more different. One was Freddie Baker's French girlfriend, Antoinette, and the other, to my considerable surprise, was Desmond Norman.

The eighty-five-year-old was doing a leisurely backstroke while Antoinette had obviously just completed her workout and was emerging from the pool. She gave me – or more probably Oscar – a friendly wave and came over to where I was standing, keeping my hand on Oscar's collar to prevent him from jumping into the pool. As the party was due to start in less than an hour, the last thing I wanted was a smelly, wet dog to further sour the already strained atmosphere among at least some of the guests.

'Hello again, Dan, and hi, Oscar. Have you tried the pool? The water temperature's perfect. Isn't this an amazing place?' Without Freddie Baker beside her, she looked and sounded decidedly more relaxed and happy.

I nodded in agreement. 'I can't think of many more charming places to have a party, although not everybody seems to be enjoying it.' The atmosphere over lunch hadn't improved, in spite of further culinary delights produced by Valentina so, seeing as I now had Antoinette to myself, I thought I might do a little bit of investigating. 'It's a pity Freddie and Jack Sloane don't get on. Is that recent, or have things always been strained between them?'

She cast an apprehensive look over her shoulder, but Norman was still in the pool and nobody else was to be seen. 'To be honest, Freddie doesn't get on well with most people.' She took another wary look around. 'I'm not sure that he likes anybody here.'

'Apart from you, of course, Antoinette.'

'Oh, yes, there's me.' The deadpan expression on her face and her lacklustre tone when she said it confirmed my suspicion that all was not well in this relationship either.

'Presumably, he likes Alice, and she likes him, otherwise he wouldn't have come, would he?'

For a moment, it looked as if she was going to say something more, but then she must have thought better of it and just nodded. 'I don't think he knows her that well. I get the feeling he only really came here because he knew there were going to be some big-name producers among the other guests, and he's always on the lookout for potential investors in his projects.' After another glance around, she added in a low voice, 'The fat man wasn't so far off the mark when he said Freddie would soon be going round knocking on doors for work. He has a habit of upsetting everybody he meets and, although he's a very good director, he's been blacklisted by a number of high-profile studios.'

Out of the corner of my eye, I spotted Desmond Norman heaving himself out of the pool. Antoinette must also have noticed as she gave me a little nod of the head and went off. I turned away, and Oscar and I continued our leisurely stroll, my mind churning. The more I discovered about this selection of guests, the more convinced I became that Alice would appear to have gone out of her way to invite the most ill-assorted group of people she could possibly have assembled. I felt sure she was an intelligent woman, so I couldn't help asking myself why she had done this. It seemed so senseless.

I explored the possible reasons she might have had, and not many presented themselves to me. First was the possibility that she was so naïve that she genuinely thought these people loved her, but I instantly dismissed that as a non-starter. I had no doubt that, after over forty years in the movie business, she would have developed keen antennae when it came to other people and their feelings towards her. If I discounted this hypothesis, what was I left with? Did she have a dark, malicious streak in her that had made her put together a group of people who disliked each other, so that she could watch them fight amongst themselves for her sport? Once again, I dismissed this idea. Of course, she was a very talented actress, and the impression I'd gained of her so far might have been an elaborate act, but I hadn't sensed anything of the kind, and I normally pick up on that sort of thing.

Ruling out the other alternative that she was going gaga and was unaware of what she was doing, I struggled to come up with an explanation until my thoughts returned to the manuscript I'd seen lying on her desk with the title *Payback*. Could it be that she had deliberately invited people who would figure in a tell-all exposé? Was she going to break the news to them that their reputations were about to be trashed? But, if so, how was she planning on doing this and why? Surely if she expected them to be annoyed, furious even, it made little sense to bring them here to her home. Of course, maybe I'd got it wrong, and what she was actually writing was a thriller. If so, I could see the logic of bringing together a group of Hollywood's movers and shakers – even if a number of them weren't her favourite people – in the hope of convincing them that her work was going to be the next big blockbuster.

I glanced down at Oscar, who was happily sniffing a statue of Venus – probably with the intention of marking it so that other dogs would know that he claimed the island as his own. I, too, knew that I wanted to do some sniffing about and I wondered which of these scenarios might be behind Alice's invitations, or if there was something I was missing. Somehow, I had the feeling the big event tonight might answer that question. When Alice had told me the evening would have a twist in the tail, had she been referring to this? Maybe tonight's murder mystery would turn out to be the prequel to *Payback*.

It promised to be an uncomfortable evening – and not just because I was going to be spending it in those damn blue tights.

13

SATURDAY EVENING

Deliberately avoiding looking at myself in the mirror, I donned my costume – including the grotesque mask – and tied the big, red ribbon onto Oscar's collar. I left my room at six with him at my side giving me suspicious looks once more. I went along the terrace to the pergola where I found that I was the first guest to arrive. The only other person out there was Diego, dressed in his medieval servant costume, preparing a table full of bottles and glasses. When he saw me, he beckoned me over.

'*Ciao*, Dan. You look good in your costume. How're the tights?'

I grimaced. 'Don't ask. I don't suppose you've got a beer, have you?'

He smiled and reached down to a cool box on the floor at his feet. 'I thought you might ask me that, so I managed to find you an authentic Renaissance-style beer mug.' His smile broadened. 'Or at least a reasonably convincing imitation.' He opened two bottles of beer and emptied them into the sturdy-looking pewter mug, roughly the size of a pint glass. 'Here you go, *cin cin*.'

I toasted him and raised the mug to my lips, inadvertently immersing the hooked nose of my mask into the beer as I did so. I snorted, wiped off the froth and pushed the mask up onto my forehead before taking a long, very welcome draught. I glanced at my watch, idly wondering if I should have taken it off for the sake of historical authenticity. 'Ten past six and nobody else here. Did I get the time wrong?'

'No, six was what Miss Graceland told everybody. I dare say they'll start arriving soon – those of them who wake up in time. They got through a lot of wine at lunchtime. Did you see how much the fat man drank?' There was awe in his voice. 'Two and a half bottles of Barolo, followed by a huge glass of grappa, and he still managed to get up and walk after that. If I drank that much, you'd have to pump me out – assuming it didn't kill me.'

I grinned. 'I've a feeling that Mr Sloane is going to cost Alice a fortune in alcohol this weekend.'

He shrugged. 'I don't think she noticed, and she probably didn't care. She had enough trouble at lunchtime today as it was.'

'Trouble? What sort of trouble, an argument?' He nodded and I shook my head ruefully. 'How weird. I was sitting at the opposite end of the long table, but surely I would have spotted something like that.'

'Two arguments, to be precise. They came right at the end of the meal, and a number of people had already left. I think it might have been after you'd gone out to give Oscar a walk. The first row was between Miss Graceland and Foster, the actor with the perfect teeth.' He shook his head in disbelief. 'I've never seen teeth that white. I wouldn't be surprised if they glow in the dark.'

'What was the row about?'

'I've no idea. My English isn't too good, and they were speaking very fast. I think it was about something that happened in the past, because he kept repeating the words "a long time ago". It only lasted a minute or so, but voices were raised on both sides.'

This chimed with what Gupta and Rodriguez had told me about the brief affair between the two actors, culminating in the explosive conclusion. But that had been over twenty years ago, and I was surprised that relations between Alice and Foster hadn't thawed in the meantime. But apparently not.

'And the other argument? Who was that with?'

'That was the old man, the one who smokes those torpedo-sized cigars. I didn't hear anything of what was said, but he was the last to get up from table and as he passed Miss Graceland, he stopped and said something to her under his breath that must have really hurt. She jumped to her feet and, for a moment, I really thought she was going to slap him but, instead, she just gritted her teeth and the two of them had what looked like a really nasty row, all conducted sotto voce. I might not have heard what was said, but it looked like one hell of a bust-up.'

I had no further time to chat to Diego as Alice herself put in an appearance. She was looking drop-dead gorgeous in her formal Renaissance costume of cream silk gown and gold mask. I hastily pulled down my mask and doffed my floppy hat as I bowed low towards her.

'Donna Alicia, good evening. May I say that you look wonderful tonight?'

Oscar at my side obviously agreed as he started wagging his tail enthusiastically.

She extended an elegant hand sheathed in a lace glove towards me and I duly kissed it. She then transferred her attention to Oscar and bent down to make a fuss of him. 'How smart you look tonight with your bow, Oscar.' I kept a close eye on him in case he might decide to jump up and make a mess of her dress, but he behaved like a true gentleman and limited himself to kissing her gloved hands just as I had done. I had a feeling he was a bit troubled by the fact that we were wearing masks, but this hadn't stopped him recognising her immediately. She straightened up again and looked around. 'My guests don't appear to be in a hurry to come and join the fun.'

'They're probably still recovering from that wonderful lunch.' There was nobody else in sight so I thought I would take a chance. 'Can I ask you something, Alice? Is it just my impression or are some of the people not exactly thrilled to be here?'

She laughed. 'What a wonderfully English way of putting it. I should have known that an expert detective like you would have picked up on that. You're quite right, there are definitely some of my guests who would rather be somewhere else.'

She was sounding quite relaxed, so I thought I would push my luck a little bit more. 'And maybe one or two of them aren't your favourite people in the whole world?'

'Right again, Sherlock.' I distinctly saw her do a full 360-degree survey of her surroundings before continuing. 'They all have one thing in common, and I bet you don't know what it is – not just that they all come from the world of showbiz.'

I decided to take a stab at it. 'I couldn't help noticing a manuscript on your desk. Might that have something to do with these people?'

She reached over and gripped my forearm. 'Selena was right. You are a great detective.' She sounded impressed. 'The answer, Dan, is yes. I hit sixty a couple of years ago, and I've taken time out to sit down and write my autobiography. And I really have written it myself. No ghostwriter for me.'

'And your guests here tonight all feature in the book?' She nodded her head, and I carried on. 'Not necessarily favourably?'

'You could say that.' Her tone was more serious now and, even though I couldn't see her face beneath her mask, I could tell that she was in the prey of powerful emotions. 'When I sat down to write my book, I knew I was going to dig up a lot of memories, and I knew that not all of them would be pleasant. The people I've invited here this weekend all play parts in my autobiography and I wanted to be able to sit down with each of them and give them a chance to explain and maybe apologise for certain things that took place. A lot of bad stuff happened in the past, and if I get the feeling that some people are genuinely sorry for what happened, then I intend to cut them out of the book and save them any embarrassment.' Her voice hardened. 'As for the ones who aren't prepared to say they're sorry, I intend to blow them out of the water. They deserve it.'

I stood there and took stock while Oscar, clearly picking up the emotion in her voice, leant against her leg and stared up at her with a concerned expression on his face. A thought occurred to me. 'What was your reasoning behind deciding to do a murder mystery weekend? Could it be that the roles you've assigned to your guests bear a resemblance to how they behaved in real life?'

'Exactly.' I couldn't see her face but I could hear satisfaction in her voice. 'Just in case they have any doubts, I've deliberately marked down on the cards that I'll be distributing in a minute some unmistakable parallels between the historical characters they'll be playing tonight and what each of them has done in real life. And for the avoidance of any doubt, I've had copies of the first draft of the manuscript made, and Mary's going to deliver them to each of the rooms in the course of this evening. By tomorrow morning, nobody's going to be under any illusions as to why they're here. That'll be when I sit down with each of them and see how they react.'

I reflected on her words. 'I would imagine it's safe to say that tomorrow's going to be an uncomfortable day for your guests and for you. In fact, I imagine the brighter guests will probably be able to work out from the cards you give them this evening what's in the back of your mind.' Remembering what Diego had just told me about the rows after lunch, I hazarded a guess. 'Or maybe some of them already have.' Not for the first time, I felt a twinge of foreboding. Hopefully, tonight's murder mystery wouldn't turn out to be a disaster – or worse.

She didn't respond but I sensed, more than saw, the slightest movement of her head indicating that I was right. I pushed my mask up onto my forehead so she could see my face, in particular my eyes. 'The next twenty-four hours are going to be very stressful for you. Are you sure you're ready for that?'

She nodded decisively. 'I'm ready.' She picked up a small envelope from the table beside her and handed it to me. 'Good luck with your investigation, Chief Inspector. I've a feeling you'll work it out. If not, here's the answer just in case.' She turned her head slightly and lowered her voice. 'Here come the first of my guests now.'

I followed the direction of her masked face and saw the unmistakable, white-haired figure of Desmond Norman approaching. He was wearing a scary black and red mask, and his clothes were all made of black satin. He could have been a medieval undertaker or a sinister jailer. It was easy to imagine him heating a red-hot poker in a brazier ready for a gruesome torture session. Reflecting back on what Alice had just told me, I couldn't help thinking that the next few hours might well turn out to be torture for at least some of the guests.

* * *

Over the course of the next hour, the guests all assembled in their costumes that ranged from the outrageously revealing and decadent gown made up of pink silk, pearls and gold thread worn by Maggie McBride, to the all-white tunic, pantaloons and tights worn by Freddie Baker, now looking considerably shorter without his ridiculous gold shoes. The women all looked very glamorous, even Lucy O'Connell, whose costume and mask conveniently concealed her worn and ravaged complexion, and whose wimple covered her unkempt hair, giving her an almost ecclesiastical look. Champagne was served, and it came as no surprise to see Jack Sloane once again doing his best to empty any bottle he found. Freddie Baker stuck to mineral water and I stuck to beer – and not too much of it. After what Alice had told me, I felt sure this was going to be an interesting evening, and I wanted to be in command of my faculties so as to observe it.

At exactly seven o'clock, Alice tapped a glass with a spoon and silence fell across the terrace. 'Ladies and gentlemen, before dinner is served, I promised that I would give you all cards with details of your characters, along with some clues for you to pass on to other guests over the course of the evening. As it's a beautiful night, we intend to serve dinner outside, and you're free to sit wherever you like. In order that you can all have the opportunity to mingle, I will ask you to change tables every now and then as the meal progresses so that by the end, you should have had the opportunity to talk to as many people as possible. Once the murder has taken place, Dan here, that's Don Daniele, the Magistrate, will gather you together and give you each the chance to offer your solution to the mystery. I hope that's clear. Now, to animate the evening, here are some other participants who have come along to help you in your investigations.'

The door to the dining room opened, and the actors trooped out one by one and, as they did so, Alice introduced them – particularly the Doge and his half-brother – to the guests. She didn't introduce the guests to the actors by name and I wondered how many of them would be recognised in the course of the evening. Hidden as they were beneath their Renaissance costumes and masks, it would be hard to identify the celebrities.

Besides, I reminded myself, the only immediately recognisable faces among the guests were probably the two actors and possibly Carlos Rodriguez and Freddie Baker, the famous directors. I presumed that the faces of the others would probably be as unfamiliar to the locally recruited actors as they had been to me.

Alice moved around among the guests, handing out individual cards to each of them. I did my best to scrutinise the people as they read what was on their cards, but the masks made it almost impossible for me to see any of the faces. There were a few exceptions. Desmond Norman, the octogenarian film producer, pushed his mask up onto his forehead and dug out a pair of reading glasses from the hidden recesses of his pantaloons, perched them on his nose and studied his card intently. As he did so, I distinctly saw him straighten up and even in the twilight beneath the arbour, as the sun headed for the horizon, I felt sure I saw his face flush. Whether this was with anger, embarrassment, or fear was impossible to tell, but clearly his opinion of our hostess hadn't improved since lunchtime.

Alastair Groves didn't remove his mask, so I couldn't see his facial features, but from the way he froze for almost a minute before raising the card to barely a few inches in front of his face so he could study it letter by letter, I had little doubt that whatever was on there had come as a considerable shock to him. His wife reached over and almost jerked it out of his hand so she could study it closely. A bit further along, I saw Carlos Rodriguez react in a similar way, holding out his card towards Greg Gupta, clearly stunned by what he'd read. The others were impossible to judge except for Jack Sloane, who also needed the assistance of reading glasses and had to remove his mask to read the card. His already flushed face turned the most unhealthy puce colour, and I saw him empty his glass in one and reach out for another from a conveniently positioned tray.

Something he had read had definitely come as a considerable shock to him.

I took a sip of beer and settled back to see what happened next. Just as it says on boxes of fireworks, *light blue touch paper and stand well clear*. The games had started – by which I mean, not only the murder mystery game, but also the far more serious one being played by our hostess.

14

SATURDAY NIGHT

A few minutes later, Valentina, her daughter and her son appeared and began to circulate with plates of nibbles. Mary, who was standing alongside me, told me that these were what the Venetians called *cicchetti*, Venice's answer to tapas. These bite-sized delicacies were amazing. There were slices of bread, some topped with bresaola, some with smoked salmon, and others with asparagus tips paired with quails' eggs. There were slices of polenta topped with melted cheese as well as grilled prawns and scallops on cocktail sticks. There were tiny grilled sausages and meatballs, served together with deep-fried soft-shell crabs. I wasn't the only one to be blown away by them. Alice made a point of accidentally on purpose dropping various titbits onto the ground in front of my ever-hungry dog, and I could almost hear him sighing with delight. I hoped his digestive system would be able to cope. I was, after all, sharing a room with him tonight.

Remembering what Alice had told me, I manoeuvred Mary over to one side, where we couldn't be overheard, and spoke quietly to her. 'I understand from Alice that you're going to be distributing some reading material later this evening. Have you had a chance to look at it?'

When she replied, her voice was little more than a whisper. 'That's why I was a bit late getting out here. Miss Graceland just gave me the manuscripts ten minutes ago. By the way, there's one there for you as well, but she's told me not to deliver them to the rooms until nine o'clock. I've just had a very quick flick through the pages, and it's what people thought it might be: her autobiography.' She leant a little closer to my ear. 'She certainly doesn't pull any punches. Assuming it's all true, this is going to cause a monumental furore in Hollywood.'

'And would I be right in thinking that the guests here tonight are her prime targets?'

She nodded. 'As I said, I've only just had ten minutes to flick through the pages, but the main names that keep coming up are standing around us right now. This book is going to be dynamite.'

I sounded a note of caution. 'Assuming she goes ahead with it. She told me this is just the first draft and she might modify it, depending on the responses she gets from her guests this weekend.'

Out of the corner of my eye, I saw Alice looking across at us, so I clinked my glass against Mary's and headed off.

While sipping my beer and helping myself to the delicious nibbles, I circulated among the guests, keen to see to what extent they were participating in the game and even keener to see how they were reacting to the contents of the cards they'd been handed. The first couple I came to were Maggie McBride and Rocco. Her cleavage was unmistakable and the striped blue and red tights that he was wearing were equally spectacular. I wandered over and toasted them with my beer mug, doing my best to get into character.

'Good evening. I am Don Daniele, the Magistrate, and this is my finest spy, Oscar. He can sniff out traitorous wretches at any distance. Tell me, what do you think of the Doge and his wife?'

Maggie McBride wasn't in the mood for play-acting. She slid her pearl-encrusted mask up onto the top of her head and glared at me. 'I'm this close to turning around and getting back on a plane to the States right now. Alice just handed me my card with my character notes on it, and there's nothing funny about what it says. Here, see for yourself.' She reached into her corsage, retrieved a small card, the size of a playing card, and handed it to me. It was still warm.

I read it carefully. There were only a few lines.

You are Donna Margherita.

You used to be a courtesan and you managed to land your-self a rich husband.

You poisoned your husband so as to inherit his fabulous wealth.

The only person who knows what you did is the Doge's wife, Donna Alicia.

You hate her and fear her in equal proportions.

Nothing would make you happier than to see her dead.

I handed back the card. As far as I could remember from what I'd read on the Internet, Maggie's husband had been thirty years older than her, and his death at the age of eighty-three hadn't come as a surprise to anybody. I certainly hadn't seen any mention of foul play. Was this just Alice spicing up the character of Donna Margherita for tonight's event, or was there more to it than that? I decided to do my best to calm Maggie down – for now.

'Alice told me last night that her character was going to be universally detested by everybody in the game. I wouldn't take it personally, if I were you. I imagine her idea is for everybody to have a motive to commit murder, and so to make it more difficult for the participants to guess who the killer is.'

Alongside her, Rocco added a few reassuring words of his own. 'Maggie, *carissima*, that's what I've been telling you. It's nothing personal. It's just a game.'

She snorted, swallowed the contents of her glass and for a moment, it looked as though she was going to hurl it to the ground, but she restrained herself and allowed Rocco to remove it from her hand and replace it with a full glass of champagne from a passing tray.

I left her fuming and moved across to another couple a bit further away. It took a moment or two for me to realise who they were beneath their masks and costumes, but I soon worked out that this had to be Alastair Groves, Alice's former agent, and his wife Sandra. She greeted me with a haughty curtsy and I was mildly surprised to see that she was entering into the spirit of the game. From what I'd seen of her so far, she hadn't struck me as having any desire to be here. Her husband, on the other hand, didn't even attempt to join in. He barely acknowledged my arrival and pointedly ignored Oscar, who looked up to me as much as to say, *What's his problem?* I concentrated my attention on Sandra Groves and gave her my Renaissance-man introduction.

'Good evening, Donna Sandra, I am Don Daniele, the Magistrate, and this is my faithful assistant, Oscar.'

She fanned herself with an elaborate paper fan decorated with wildflowers. 'Good evening, Don Daniele. I'm pleased to see you.' Her tone was at odds with her words, but at least she had responded, which was more than could be said for her husband. 'You're the detective, aren't you?'

I nodded. 'That's correct. Unlike everybody else, I haven't been given a card telling me who I am, who I hate, or giving me any clues as to the identity of the murderer. I imagine you and your husband both received a card?'

I saw her head jerk around towards her husband for a second. With the mask covering her face, I couldn't tell what she was thinking, but, from what I'd seen earlier, I had little doubt that the contents of his card had caused him the same seismic jolt that had rocked Maggie McBride. What, I wondered, was the skeleton in his cupboard?

Sandra Groves turned back towards me and answered, but her dislike for the island, her hostess and the game was all too evident in her voice as she did so. 'Yes, but this whole charade strikes me as so terribly juvenile, don't you think so, Alastair?'

In response, he gave a sullen growl, not dissimilar to the sort of noise Oscar makes when he thinks there might be a squirrel lurking close by. Fortunately, at that moment, I spotted the unmistakable figure of Jack Sloane in the process of helping himself to more champagne, and I excused myself and walked over to see him. His mask was up on the top of his head, but he had squeezed himself into a voluminous yellow tunic and tights and, as a result, he bore a distinct resemblance to *Sesame Street*'s Big Bird. Given his already fairly grumpy behaviour, I didn't bother with the Renaissance stuff.

'Good evening, Mr Sloane. Are you looking forward to the murder mystery?'

'Murder mystery my...' The sentence disintegrated into an unprintable litany of invective, and I acted surprised.

'Surely it'll be fun.'

He glared at me – and at the world in general. 'Fun? If I'd known what that little bitch was planning, I would never have come.'

Still trying to appear clueless, I queried his choice of vocabulary. 'When you say, "that little bitch", are you talking about Alice?'

'Who the hell else would I be talking about? You know what she's done? Do you… do you?' I was glad I was wearing my mask, because the alcohol on his breath risked burning the paint off it as he leant belligerently in my direction. 'She's given me a card on which it says I'm a rapist. I never raped nobody. Any woman says that, she's lying.' The fury in his eyes was tempered by an expression I recognised only too well: it was fear. Fear of being found out, maybe? Fear of a distant memory being dug up and flung at him? Beneath the insults and the bluster, I felt sure that Jack Sloane was a worried man. I produced a few comments along the lines of it only being a game, and for him not to take things personally, before I headed off. I noticed that Oscar didn't hang about either.

Over the next half-hour, I managed to exchange a few words with all of the main players, and the only ones that sounded reasonably unaffected were Greg Gupta and, unexpectedly, Lucy O'Connell. Of all of us, Gupta was the one who managed to pull off the Renaissance look most successfully. His predominantly grey and black striped costume gave him a rakish air, and he had the best legs of all of us – the men at least. Lucy O'Connell in her wimple that covered her whole head apart from her face – and that was concealed beneath a full face mask – cast a somewhat forlorn figure, and it occurred to me that the choice of costume neatly encapsulated her present condition. Whether she was still on drugs was impossible to tell, but, from what I'd seen of her at lunchtime, she was in need of some serious rehab to return her to her former beautiful self.

The three of us chatted for a couple of minutes, and I was pleasantly surprised to hear Lucy O'Connell sounding unexpectedly animated. Hopefully, this excitement had been brought about by the prospect of the murder mystery rather than by pharmaceutical means. Both of them told me they had received cards from Alice, but neither spoke of their contents, so they were either quite literally keeping their cards close to their chests, or there hadn't been anything as contentious on their cards as on those given to some of the other guests.

We were joined a few minutes later by Carlos Rodriguez. Even with his mask on, I could almost feel the indignation emanating from the famous director, and I couldn't help wondering what his card had said. Did he have a guilty secret and, if so, what might it be?

At that moment, we were invited to sit down for dinner and I joined the three of them at a table under the vine-covered pergola. At the next table, Alice and Mary were accompanied by the actor playing the part of the Doge and nobody else. Clearly, the comments on the cards hadn't endeared the hostess to the majority of her guests.

'Would you mind if I join you?' The strong Yorkshire accent was unmissable, and I looked up to see the impressive figure of the actor playing the part of Admiral Diodato. We waved him into a spare seat and he immediately launched into the murder mystery plot.

'The word on the street – or should I say in the canal? – is that there's going to be an attempt on the life of the Doge this evening.' He glanced in my direction. 'Don Daniele, have your spies been telling you the same thing?'

I played along with him. 'From what I've heard, Admiral, there's a very real threat to somebody here on this island and, of course, you know what that means, don't you? That means that the would-be killer is almost certainly sitting at one of these tables right now, maybe even at this very table.'

The Admiral nodded in agreement. 'Exactly. Nobody is free

from suspicion. Why, Don Daniele, the murderer might even be you.'

'Indeed, and the same applies to you. My spies have told me that there's no love lost between you and the Doge, or his lady wife. Are you carrying a weapon?'

He shook his head. 'No, your men confiscated our knives when we arrived on the island. If there's going to be a murder, the killer will have to use one of these.' He picked up a pointed steak knife from the table in front of him and held it up threateningly. 'Somebody here tonight might well use this to commit a murder. It's a sobering thought.'

On that note, he grabbed his glass and swallowed the last of his champagne before turning towards me again and dropping the 'Renaissance man' act for a moment. 'How did you manage to get yourself a beer? I'm gasping for one.'

I stayed in character. 'In my business, Admiral, it pays to know people.' I imagined he could hear the humour in my voice even through my mask and I added sotto voce, 'If you like, I can have a word with Diego on your behalf.'

A moment or two later, I saw Diego's daughter emerge from the kitchen carrying a large wooden tray with three steaming silver dishes on it. She came over to our table and explained what was on offer. 'The cook has prepared three different pasta dishes and she suggests that you might like to try all three.' She set the tray down on the table and pointed to the dishes one after the other. '*Bigoli ai frutti di mare, tagliatelle al ragù* and *lasagne al forno*.' She started with the Admiral. 'Admiral Diodato, would you like to try them all?'

He raised his mask and gave Gabriella a broad smile before answering her in perfect Italian, interestingly without even a hint of his Yorkshire accent. 'Do you need to ask? Yes, please, it smells divine.' His smile broadened even further when I managed to attract Diego's attention and a tankard of beer was presented to the Admiral.

Gabriella went around the table serving the pasta, which did indeed smell absolutely amazing, and I was pleased to see Lucy O'Connell accept a reasonable-sized plateful. She was pitifully thin, and I felt sure what she needed was good food, rest and the chance to recover. Her arms were bare and I couldn't miss faint bruising on the inside of her elbow and forearm, although it looked as though she had tried to conceal it. I felt genuinely sorry for her. This might mean that she hadn't kicked the habit yet, and I wondered idly how she had dared to smuggle class A drugs through Customs. For a celebrity, it would have been a high-risk strategy unless she had somehow arranged to pick them up here in Venice. I remembered what Virgilio's inspector friend had told me. There was no shortage of drugs to be found in Venice.

15

SATURDAY NIGHT

In the course of the next hour, we all changed places three or four times, and I found myself speaking to most of the guests and to all of the actors. I didn't get the chance to speak to Alice, but I was pleased to see at least some of the guests interacting with her as the meal progressed. Darkness fell and Valentina set candles on the tables under the pergola, giving the night a romantic air.

Any trace of romance disappeared at just after nine-thirty, when there was a sudden crash. Oscar jumped to his feet and my eyes followed the direction of his pointing nose. At the next table but one, a lone figure was slumped forward, face down, with a wine bottle lying smashed on the floor alongside. Even from this distance, the blonde hair, the golden mask and the cream gown were unmistakable. Alice, AKA Donna Alicia, the Doge's wife, had been murdered.

It was time for the Magistrate to get to work.

I got to my feet and walked across, taking charge of the situation. I moved everybody away from the table, just as if it were a real murder, leaving Alice slumped with her head on her hands, apparently dead. I toyed with the idea of letting my hand press against the carotid artery in her neck as I had done numerous times in my career as a detective, but I decided that, as this was only a game, the audience would just have to take my word for it that she was dead. I turned towards the assembled guests. There was an expectant silence, broken only by the distant sound of an aircraft coming in to land at Marco Polo airport.

'Ladies and gentlemen, I have grave news.' I did my best to act the part. 'Donna Alicia, the wife of our beloved Doge, has been murdered, and the killer has to be here among us now.' I took off my mask and let my eyes run across the terrace as I addressed them all. 'Fortunately, I know that you will all now do your best to solve this case for me. Has anybody any theories about who might have committed this foul deed?'

The actor playing the part of the Doge stood up and pointed an accusing finger at his half-brother's wife. 'I know it was you, Donna Eleonora. You killed my beloved wife.' He looked over in my direction. 'Magistrate, how was she killed?'

I had been wondering about this. Had this been a real murder, I would have ordered a forensic team to come and establish the facts, but as this was a game, I did a bit of invention. 'It looks to me, Your Excellency, as if she has been poisoned.'

The Doge nodded slowly. 'I wonder if the poison was intended for her or for me. If it was poison, then I could just as easily have eaten or drunk whatever it was that has killed her. I was sitting alongside her only a few minutes ago.' He spun around once more and pointed his finger in the direction of his half-brother's wife again. 'It was you. I know it was you.'

I thanked him for his intervention and threw it open to the guests.

Greg Gupta was the next to stand up. He appeared to have no doubt about the identity of the culprit, but it wasn't Donna Eleonora. He walked over to the table where Mary was sitting and laid his hand upon her shoulder. 'The last person I saw sitting with the Doge and his wife was this young lady, his personal secretary. She was best placed to poison the food on the table, so it must have been her.'

I looked around at the other guests. 'A murder needs a motive. What motive might this young woman have had for killing her employer?'

Mary jumped to her feet and did a convincing job of denying any involvement in the murder. This was followed by a variety of accusations and rebuttals from a number of guests, although at least half of them didn't bother even to hazard a guess. I assumed that they were still furious with Alice and had no intention of playing by her rules. Jack Sloane was still sitting at a table by himself – as far as I could tell, he hadn't moved an inch all evening – with no fewer than three wine bottles in front of him – two of them empty – and on the other side of the terrace, Lucy O'Connell had also chosen a table on her own. Neither of them took any part in solving the mystery and appeared lost in their own little worlds – in Sloane's case, a highly alcoholic one. Oscar must have worked out that Lucy O'Connell wasn't doing too well as he had wandered over to position himself alongside her and I saw her fondling his ears with her hand. Hopefully, he would be able to bring some cheer into her life.

I gave the guests ten minutes or so of accusations and counteraccusations before I decided the time had come to wrap things up. I genuinely had no idea whatsoever who had committed the murder and I was reaching for the sealed envelope in the pocket of my tunic for the solution when something suddenly struck me. Alice had told me that the murder mystery would have a twist in the tail. In other words, she had planned things so that everybody would be surprised, and it occurred to me that I might know what she had had in mind. It was Oscar that gave it away.

Ever since he'd met Alice, he'd been obsessed with her, and her generous distribution of tasty nibbles to him in the course of this evening had only cemented their relationship further. As a result, he had spent most of the meal either sitting alongside me, or more often positioned beside Alice, looking up at her adoringly – and receiving yet more food in return for his idolatry. And yet, he had now transferred his attention to the lonely figure of Lucy O'Connell.

Or had he?

I called the proceedings to order.

'Right, ladies and gentlemen, I think it's time we solved this murder.' As I spoke, I walked through the tables across to where Lucy O'Connell was sitting with Oscar at her side and I stopped when I reached her table. 'Here, ladies and gentlemen, unless I'm very much mistaken, you will find the ever-resourceful wife of the Doge, whose cunning ruse has allowed her to avoid assassination.' I pointed at the figure in Lucy O'Connell's costume. 'Would you like to stand up and tell everybody the truth, *Donna Alicia*?'

I was gratified to hear at least a couple of gasps of surprise behind me and even more gratified to see the figure dressed in Lucy O'Connell's clothes slowly stand up and reach for her mask. She pulled it off and revealed what I had suspected. Alice had swapped clothes and masks with Lucy, so as to confound the murderer and her guests, and there was even a little ripple of applause. At this point, I decided to hand over the big reveal to the party organiser.

'And now, Donna Alicia, it's over to you to tell us exactly what happened. Who just tried – and failed – to murder you?'

She headed for the centre of the terrace and as she passed me, she murmured quietly in my ear, 'Selena said you were good.' She stopped when she reached the middle of the group of guests and launched into her explanation. It was a bit tortuous, and I had a feeling that the logic wouldn't have stood up to close scrutiny in a court of law, but everybody listened, most of them apparently riveted, as she revealed that the murderer had in fact been the character played by Dirk Foster. He, Don Dirco, had once had a relationship with the Doge's wife that had ended when he'd been unfaithful to her. Since then, he had lived in fear of her taking her revenge against him and had chosen to strike first, before she could tarnish his reputation.

I studied the faces around me as she related the backstory that so closely reflected the events that had really happened in Alice's past. As the murder mystery was now over, most of the guests had removed their masks, and I was able to observe their reactions to this story. Quite clearly, it didn't come as such a surprise to at least some of them. As for Dirk Foster, his face displayed a range of emotions from outrage and anger to something more akin to embarrassment and, before Alice had even finished talking, he leapt to his feet and disappeared into the dark. His departure was followed by another ripple of applause led by Greg Gupta, who stood up and walked over to where Lucy O'Connell was still playing the part of the murdered woman.

'It's all right, Lucy, you can straighten up now. The big bad wolf's gone.' He touched Lucy's shoulder and immediately stepped back with a shocked expression on his face, casting a despairing look in my direction. 'Something bad's happened. Something very bad.'

I hurried across and did what I had almost done fifteen minutes earlier. I placed my finger against the side of her throat in search of a pulse but found nothing. I tried again, but still without success. My mind was racing. The premonition I had been feeling had been justified. The murder mystery game had suddenly become a real murder. It was a struggle to get my head round what had just happened. Finally, accepting the inevitable, I straightened up and turned around slowly. 'I'm afraid it looks as though she's dead.'

There was a boo from the far side of the terrace. 'Damn actors, always trying to milk it. Cut, sweetheart, cut. Your scene's over.' Jack Sloane's slurred voice was unmistakable, and his comment raised a few sardonic laughs.

I held up my hands to quell the merriment. 'I'm afraid I'm not joking. This is for real. Lucy O'Connell is dead.' I took out a tissue and used it as I gently loosened and removed her mask. The blank, staring eyes on the tabletop told their own story, and I heard gasps from several of those closest to the table. In case there were still any doubters, I lifted the convincing blonde wig from her head, revealing her short hair beneath. The jocular mood across the terrace died, and I turned and searched the shadows for Diego or Valentina. Spotting them over by the kitchen door, I called across to them.

'Contact the emergency services now – police and ambulance.' As they stood there, rooted to the spot, I raised the intensity in my voice. 'A woman's dead. Call them. *Now!*'

As Diego turned and scuttled back indoors, I set about securing the crime scene – if, indeed, it had been a crime. A drug addict ending up dead didn't always imply foul play. Maybe Lucy had overdosed. Automatically, as I'd done so many times before, I did my best to memorise where everybody had been seated, wishing I'd thought to tuck my notebook in my pantaloons. I called Valentina over and asked her if she could organise some coffees and maybe something a little stronger for anybody who felt the need. I positioned her son and daughter several metres from the victim with instructions to ensure that nobody came any closer than that. Once I was certain that nobody was going to interfere with the crime scene, I walked over to where Alice was still standing, motionless. Her face was deadly pale. I recognised the signs of shock and took her arm, leading her to a seat, where she collapsed in a heap and looked up despairingly at me.

'That could have been me, Dan. Whoever did that thought they were killing *me*.' There was abject terror in her voice, and I did my best to reassure her – for now.

'At this stage, we don't know whether Lucy really has been murdered, Alice. She was a drug addict. You know that, don't you? Maybe it was self-inflicted. The police will be here soon and they'll get to the bottom of it. Please try not to worry.' Automatically, as I had done many times in my career, I tried to sound as comforting as possible although, deep down, my gut was telling me that something far worse than suicide had just taken place here.

Predictably, Oscar positioned himself at Alice's side again with his nose on her knee, doing his best to add a bit of canine support. She looked as if she needed it but, I reminded myself, she was a very talented actor, after all. The brutal truth was that if Lucy O'Connell really had been murdered, her killer was almost certainly one of the people close by me right now.

And nobody was above suspicion.

16

SATURDAY NIGHT

The police arrived barely twenty minutes later. I half-expected to see Virgilio's friend, Inspector Giulia Trevisan, but the first to arrive were a sergeant and two constables, closely followed by an ambulance boat with two paramedics and a doctor.

Diego showed the doctor to the victim, and it took little more than a few seconds for her to pronounce Lucy O'Connell dead. No sooner had she stepped away from the body than the sergeant and his men began to move in. I was appalled to see that none of them were wearing gloves and I couldn't stop myself from remonstrating with them.

'Sergeant, you do realise that this could be murder, don't you? Shouldn't you be wearing gloves and preferably overalls?'

He turned and looked me up and down with an exasperated expression. He was probably around my age, and one look at his face told me that I was wasting my time if I hoped he would listen to me. In case I was in any doubt, he went on to tell me as much. 'Thank you, sir, but I don't need advice from members of the public. I've seen this kind of thing often enough in my career. For your information, it's clear to me that this wasn't murder. The victim was a drug addict. Anybody can see that.' He pointed at Lucy's pathetically thin arms. 'See that bruising? That's typical of addicts. This person has died of an overdose, and I'd be grateful if you would step back and let me get on with my job.'

I've always had an obstinate streak – ask my ex-wife – and I wasn't going to stand by and see a crime scene contaminated by a trio of heavy-handed coppers, so I tried again, this time addressing myself to the doctor.

'Doctor, is the officer right? Because if he isn't, his boss is going to be very unhappy at him for contaminating a crime scene.' I deliberately made my voice loud enough for the three police officers to hear. 'Is it possible that the victim was murdered?'

I was relieved to see her step back towards the body again, studying it more closely. 'The sergeant could well be right about the victim being a drug addict, but there's no way of knowing whether that's what killed her until we do an autopsy. Certainly, if you're putting me on the spot and asking me to tell you whether it was misadventure or murder, I can't do that.'

We both looked across at the sergeant expectantly. I could tell that he was peeved – and on one level, I didn't blame him. After all, who was this nobody, trying to teach him his job? Seeing him looking uncertain, I decided to play my joker.

'Why not give Inspector Trevisan a call and see what she says? It can't hurt.'

His expression became more wary. 'How do you know Inspector Trevisan?'

'She's a friend, and I had coffee with her yesterday. I used to be a *commissario* in the police myself.' I didn't mention in which force. Sensing that I was getting through to him, I did my best to offer him a face-saving way out. 'The fact is that things here have been very fraught, and I have good reason to believe that foul play may have been involved.' I gave him a little smile. 'I'm sorry, I probably should have told you that earlier.'

He nodded a couple of times before turning to the other two officers. 'Pavan, Piave, stay here and make sure nobody touches a thing, while I call the station.' He walked off, reaching for his phone.

I went over to where Alice was still sitting motionless and I leant against the table in front of her. I'd been speaking in Italian with the police and so she probably hadn't understood what had been said. Indeed, most probably few, if any, of the guests would have understood either, so I raised my voice a bit when I spoke to her, ensuring that the others would hear.

'The sergeant is going to phone the police station so that a more senior officer can be sent out to take charge. I imagine that a forensic team will come at the same time, and we should find out before too long the exact cause of Lucy's death. We probably all know that she had a drug problem so it might be an accidental, or even a deliberate, overdose, but we have to face the fact that it's possible that she's been murdered. I'm afraid this is probably going to mean that everybody here on the island, including you and me, Alice, will have to be interviewed, and the police will probably want to take our fingerprints and maybe even DNA samples for exclusion purposes. I have a feeling it might turn out to be a long night.'

Alice slowly looked up from Oscar at her feet, and I could see the anguish in her face. 'What you're saying, Dan, is that if she was murdered, it must have been one of us who did it.'

I tried to play this down for now, although the exact same thoughts were running through my head. 'Not necessarily, but don't let's get ahead of ourselves. We should let the police and the forensic people do their work first, and then we'll know better.'

'And if she was murdered, it was because of my stupid game,

and poor Lucy was killed by mistake, and it's my fault. There's no doubt in my mind that I was the target. Whoever did this to Lucy was trying to kill *me*, and what worries me most of all is whether they'll try again.'

There was a muted chorus of dissenting voices as a few people did their best to reassure her that she had nothing to worry about but, deep down, I felt sure that she was right.

Valentina and Gabriella emerged from the kitchen with trays of strong coffee, and I helped myself to one while unobtrusively studying the faces around me. Apart from the serving staff, I counted Alice and ten guests – Dirk Foster hadn't returned after storming off – plus Mary and the six actors engaged for the game. For now, I mentally discounted the actors because I was at a loss to think of what possible motive any of them might have had to murder Lucy O'Connell. I also sidelined Mary, Valentina, Diego and their children for the same reason.

This left me with Alice herself – although at this stage, I had no idea why she might have wanted to kill Lucy – and her guests, few, if any, of whom could have realised that the woman in Alice's costume had in fact been Lucy. From what I'd seen over the last twelve hours, Alice certainly wasn't flavour of the month with a number of these, but the question was whether one of them might have decided to take the radical step of trying to kill her. As far as I could tell at the moment, the only guests not out for Alice's blood were probably Rocco Gentile, Sandra Groves – although she hadn't exactly sounded enchanted to be here – Antoinette Latour and Greg Gupta. This left me with six possible suspects here, plus Dirk Foster, who had gone off in a huff.

These were Desmond Norman, the all-powerful producer, Jack Sloane, the casting director, Maggie McBride, the widowed billionaire producer, Carlos Rodriguez, the famous director, Alastair Groves, the theatrical agent, and Freddie Baker, the new-kidon-the-block director. I had seen all of them react angrily – or at least suspiciously – at what Alice had written on their cards, except for Freddie Baker. I hadn't observed his reaction but I had sensed a certain degree of antipathy between him and Alice when he'd first appeared in the dining room at lunchtime. According to Diego, Dirk Foster and Desmond Norman had crossed swords with Alice after lunch, and her deliberate choice to make Foster the murderer and to spell out in her summing-up the way his Renaissance character had betrayed hers had led to him going off. As a result, I tended to position him high up on my list of suspects, with Norman not far behind.

My thoughts were interrupted as Dirk Foster reappeared on the terrace, changed back into his everyday clothes, with his suitcase in one hand. He ignored Alice completely, spotted Diego and waved to summon him. 'I need to get off this island. I want you to take me across to the old town or the mainland. Right now!' He was still looking and sounding furious. I saw the two police officers eyeing each other. I wondered how much English they understood, and if they had already recognised him as the world-famous star he was, but it was clear they were unsure what his intentions were. I hurried across to put Foster in the picture.

'I'm afraid you aren't going anywhere, Mr Foster. None of us are.' I pointed across to the two police officers. 'Lucy O'Connell's dead.'

This stopped him in his tracks, and he dropped his suitcase onto the ground with a thud. 'Lucy dead? But how...?'

I told him briefly that a police investigation would establish the cause of death and that it was uncertain at this stage whether we were looking at an accident, suicide or murder. 'I'm afraid we'll all have to stay here at least for tonight. A senior police officer is coming out to the island now, and I imagine he or she will want to take statements from everybody.'

He stared at me blankly for a couple of seconds. 'Did you say murder? Do the police think she was murdered? And if so, who by?' He looked and sounded convincing, but I couldn't help reminding myself that he also was a very good actor. Besides, was his bewilderment because he had just discovered that he had killed the wrong woman? I told him how Alice had swapped costumes with the victim and so maybe Alice had been the intended victim, and his tanned face paled visibly. He pulled out a chair and sat down heavily, waving vaguely towards Valentina and muttering, 'Coffee.'

I left him to his coffee and went over to explain to the two police officers that Foster hadn't been present when the victim's death had been discovered, so this had apparently come as a very unwelcome surprise to him. I stood alongside them for a minute or two, studying the crime scene. The impact of the victim's head on the table had tipped over a glass and a wine bottle, and a trail of red wine showed the track of the bottle as it had rolled off the table to smash on the ground by Lucy's feet. The overturned glass still had a little puddle of red wine left in it, and I felt sure that this would be worth careful investigation. There was one other wine glass on the table, but it was empty, and in front of the body were the remains of a half-eaten bowl of the excellent fruit salad Valentina had prepared as a healthy alternative to the no fewer than three different cakes, tarts and puddings she had served as dessert. If I'd been the investigating officer, I would have directed Forensics to study the fruit salad most carefully as well as the wine residue.

A matter of minutes later, the next wave of police officers arrived, and this time, I was secretly pleased to see it headed by Inspector Giulia Trevisan, with the sergeant by her side. She was accompanied by half a dozen other officers, some already wearing forensic overalls, and it looked as though they were now giving Lucy's death the serious investigation it merited. When the sergeant led the inspector over to me, she held out her hand. I shook it but, before she could say anything, I was determined to get in a few words first.

'Good evening, Inspector. It's good to see you again, but it's a pity about the circumstances.' I used the polite form of the pronoun 'you', although she and I had happily used the familiar form the previous day. 'I fully understand that, like everybody else here on the island, if it turns out to be murder, I'm a potential suspect, so if you want me to retreat into the background, just say the word.'

She gave me a little smile. 'Let's wait until we know one way or the other, Dan. In the meantime, there's no need for you to be so formal.' To make the point, she was using the familiar form of 'you'. 'While the pathologist and his team get on with their work, why don't we find somewhere we can sit down, and you can tell me what you meant when you told Sergeant Scarpa that things here on the island had been "fraught"?'

I led her and the sergeant along the terrace until we came to a couple of benches positioned outside the greenhouse, a fine old-fashioned, cast-iron lamp illuminating our surroundings. We sat down opposite each other and I didn't waste any time.

'The island belongs to Alice Graceland and the victim's name is Lucy O'Connell.' I saw recognition on the faces of both officers. 'That's right, two of the biggest stars in the movie business. Lucy O'Connell had gone downhill fast in the past few years and I'm almost certain she was a long-term drug addict, so it's very possible, as the sergeant quite rightly pointed out, that her death has been the result of an overdose. However, the situation here on the island has been awkward, to say the least, for completely different reasons.'

I went on to give them a breakdown of what I'd learned over

the last twenty-four hours, particularly Alice's intention to confront the people featured in her autobiography, against whom she bore a grudge. I ran through the list of guests, actors and staff here on the island, and both officers made copious notes as I provided a brief description of each of the guests. Giulia Trevisan whistled under her breath as I reeled off their job titles.

'Wow, it sounds like we have half the movers and shakers in Hollywood here. When the media get wind of this – and I'll do everything I can to see that they don't – there's going to be all hell to pay.' She gave me a helpless smile. 'By which I mean that Scarpa and I are going to have our superiors breathing down our necks.' She glanced across at him. 'Thank God you've done everything by the book so far.'

The sergeant shot me a sheepish look, and I gave him a smile and a wink in return, before continuing with my account of tonight's murder mystery. I started by mentioning the cards handed out by Alice that had caused such outrage among at least some of the guests. I related what Alice had said about the character played by Dirk Foster in the murder mystery and his incandescent reaction, and she immediately instructed the sergeant to collect all the cards, making a careful note of which had been given to whom, and she added a direct command.

'First things first, Scarpa, I want you to make sure that every officer, every paramedic, the doctor, any sailors or crew, all get the message that anything or anybody they've seen here tonight is strictly classified information. If anybody so much as mutters a word about who's here on the island, I'll see that they regret it. Make sure that the message is understood. I mean it. Not a word to anybody.'

As the sergeant jumped to his feet, a thought occurred to me. 'How's your English, Sergeant? Would you like me to give you a helping hand?'

He shook his head. 'My English isn't too good, but it should be sufficient for this. Thanks for the offer but, if need be, I can ask one of the serving staff to help me with the translation.'

After he'd disappeared along the terrace, Giulia leant forward towards me. 'Thanks for making sure Scarpa called me in. With big names like these involved, this case is going to come under a lot of scrutiny.'

I smiled back at her. 'No problem. The thing is, the sergeant might well be right about it being an overdose, but with all the background jealousies and anger bubbling away here, I felt it was better to be safe than sorry. By the way, you told me your English wasn't particularly fluent, so if you'd like me to help with interpreting, I'm at your service.'

'Thanks, Dan, I might take you up on that, but probably not until tomorrow. All I need for now is to check through the list of who's here, and for the pathologist to work overtime to establish the exact cause of death. If it turns out to be suspicious, then I'll be back first thing in the morning to take statements from everybody. I'll give orders that nobody is to leave the island until I say so.'

I nodded approvingly. 'Sounds very sensible. What I can do in the meantime is to take a quick look through Alice Graceland's book.' In response to a raised eyebrow from the inspector, I explained. 'A copy of the first draft of the manuscript of her autobiography has been delivered to each of the guests this evening, including to me, and I can't wait to take a look at it. Certainly, if Lucy O'Connell's death turns out to be suspicious, I feel pretty strongly that the murderer's real target must have been Alice Graceland and, depending on what she says about each individual guest in her book, that might help us establish who had the strongest motive for trying to murder her.'

17

SATURDAY NIGHT / SUNDAY MORNING

As soon as Oscar and I got back to my room, I spotted the manuscript lying on my bed. It had been copied and spiral bound, and I wondered if this had been in the package that Diego had had to pick up the previous day. There was even a colour cover, with a picture, not of the author as I might have expected, but simply of a plate with the remains of a meal on it and the title *Payback*. The strapline underneath read, *A dish best served cold*. It was a bleak image, and I had a feeling I was going to find that what lay beneath the cover would be equally bleak.

It was almost eleven o'clock when I started reading, and I finally had to stop at just after three in the morning. This was for two reasons: firstly, because my eyes were starting to close and secondly, and more urgently, because Oscar's dietary excesses of the last twenty-four hours had started to catch up with him, and his ominously rumbling tummy told me that he and I would do well to go out in the fresh air. We went outside and I closed the door quietly behind me, expecting to find everybody on the island fast asleep. Instead, I saw that there were lights on in three of the bedrooms and I could hear muffled voices further along the terrace under the pergola. I had a feeling that the midnight oil was being burnt by the guests as they leafed through Alice's book, searching for references to themselves. I took Oscar the long way around the garden and, while we walked, I reflected on what I'd been reading.

In many cases, Alice had opted not to name names, but the descriptions she gave meant the various people who cropped up in the course of the book were fairly easy to identify. Many of the people she mentioned received very favourable treatment from her, and I actually found myself smiling at some of the anecdotes. Given the circumstances, however, I skipped quickly through the happy chapters and concentrated on those relating to events in Alice's past that were anything but happy. The majority of these dated back to the years when she had been starting out in show business and, given the recent Hollywood scandals involving lecherous movie execs with their infamous casting couches, I was unsurprised, but still appalled, to read her accounts of deplorable incidents in her past.

One of these involved somebody described by her as 'the most powerful man in Hollywood'. This man, some twenty-five years older than her and far from attractive, had invited her up to his rooms, where he had made her a proposition. It made my skin creep to read the matter-of-fact way in which she recounted that he had told her quite openly that if she had sex with him, he would give her a part in a movie. According to her book, she had refused and left, but she hadn't fared so well with another man the following year. This man was described as being *a heavily overweight character over ten years older than me, and the man they called the star-maker*. When she had visited his office, he had insisted that she strip to her underwear – 'so I can see your figure' – and then, in spite of her attempts to defend herself, he had sexually assaulted her.

The identities of these two men were all too easy to work out. Desmond Norman was twenty-three years older than Alice, and he had very definitely been all-powerful – and probably still was. Jack Sloane, the casting director, was thirteen years older than her, and he fitted the description of the heavily overweight star-maker perfectly. Reading the accounts of her ordeals at their hands, I could well understand why she might be longing for revenge.

Carlos Rodriguez, described in her book simply as 'a well-known Latino movie director', had apparently refused to cast her in a leading role in one of his most successful movies, telling Alice's agent that she was 'too old and too unprofessional for the part'. Considering that she was over ten years younger than him and with decades of experience, this must have really hurt, but why had he been so mean? I got the distinct feeling that there was something here that wasn't being said.

The most mysterious one of all was her former agent, easily identified as Alastair Groves. Nowhere did Alice specify what he'd done, but she indicated that she had had no choice but to sack him, in spite of his having been instrumental in building and developing her career. The only explanation she gave – if indeed it could be called an explanation – was, *He knows what he did.*

The whole of chapter seven was devoted to her whirlwind romance with Dirk Foster twenty-five years earlier, and it confirmed that, just like his character in the murder mystery, he had been unfaithful to her and she had dumped him as a result. But the bombshell was the identity of the woman with whom he had hooked up. This woman, born within a few days of Alice, was described as *a little tart with dyed blonde hair, who slept her way around the USA until she finally managed to hook herself a real live billionaire – a bit long in the tooth, but loaded.* This would appear to explain why Maggie McBride had been invited to the party.

I had been speed-reading most of the time, but I had been unable to find anything negative about Lucy O'Connell – in fact, I sensed real affection in the description Alice gave of this unfortunate victim of the Hollywood jungle. Nor could I find any mention of Greg Gupta or Wilfred Baker but, considering that it was a three hundred-page manuscript, I could easily have missed them.

Once Oscar and I had walked around to the other side of the garden, I climbed up a set of steps onto the top of the wall and paused to ponder what all this meant. The lights of the old city twinkled in the distance and, in spite of the hour, I was surprised to see the green and red navigation lights of a number of vessels moving across the lagoon. Clearly, Venice was a city that never fully slept. Oscar sat down beside me and started yawning. I knew how he felt. I knew I really should be in bed, because I felt sure that tomorrow, or rather today as it already was, was going to be busy. I tried to concentrate on the case, but I could feel my eyelids drooping so I glanced down at Oscar.

'Well, dog, who do you think did it?'

He yawned again and looked up with an expression that clearly indicated that this would be up to me to work out, but first, of course, we had to discover whether poor Lucy O'Connell really had been murdered or whether she had taken her own life.

* * *

I was woken by somebody knocking on my door at just after seven-thirty in the morning. Under normal circumstances, I would already have been up by this time, but upon returning to my room with Oscar in the middle of the night, I had stripped off and gone out like a light. I wrapped a towel around my waist and padded across to open the door. To my surprise, it was Alice. She looked as if she'd just stepped out of a beauty parlour, her make-up, hair and clothes perfect. I took a couple of steps back and waved apologetically in the direction of my bare torso.

'Sorry I'm not dressed. I spent most of the night reading your book.'

She smiled at me, a slightly nervous smile, and came into the room, closing the door carefully behind her. 'Hi, Dan, sorry to wake you, but I need your advice.'

By this time, Oscar had realised that he was being visited by his new best friend, and I left the two of them happily making a fuss of each other while I grabbed some clothes and ducked into the bathroom to pull on shorts and a T-shirt. When I emerged, I found Oscar sprawled on his back, all four legs in the air, sweeping the floor with his tail, while Alice tickled his tummy. She was sitting on the edge of the bed, so I opted to sit on a nearby chair. She gave Oscar one last pat and then straightened up.

'Dan, do you think Lucy was murdered?'

'I honestly don't know. As far as I could see, she might well have still been on drugs. Do you think that's possible?'

Alice nodded. 'It's all so terribly sad. She'd been in rehab for months, and I really thought she was getting somewhere, until I got word from a friend two weeks ago that she'd checked herself out and was shooting herself full of that stuff again. I've always had a soft spot for her, so I invited her to come here and stay for as long as it was going to take. I persuaded Desmond Norman to give her a lift in his jet, so it couldn't have been easier for her. The idea was that she would have a bit of company for a couple of days with everybody else here, but then they would leave, and she and I could settle down to a quiet routine in a place where she wouldn't constantly be pestered by drug dealers or other addicts.' She looked up and I could see tears glistening in her eyes. 'And now, of course, that's all gone out of the window.'

I gave her a few moments to compose herself before I asked the question that had been preying on my mind. 'Do you think it might have been a deliberate overdose? Might she have been trying to take her own life?'

Alice shook her head. 'No way. She and I spent most of yesterday afternoon together, and she was telling me how she was determined to really make a go of it this time. She bitterly regretted falling off the wagon again and she said she was doing all she could to get her life back on track. She claimed she'd been clean for over a week now. I'm sure addicts say that sort of thing all the time, but I got the impression that she really meant it.'

I tried another question. 'Might she have overdosed by mistake?'

Alice paused for thought. 'I suppose anything's possible. I don't know much about drugs, particularly not hard drugs, but surely somebody who's shooting up on a regular basis is unlikely to make that kind of mistake.'

This didn't really accord with my experience of drug addicts, but I said nothing. Instead, I queried what had brought her to my room at this early hour, and she explained.

'You said you've been reading my book. I don't know how far into it you've managed to get, but I imagine you've identified a number of the people who're here now. I suppose any one of them would be delighted to see me dead, and I've spent all night wondering just who might have been so outraged that they decided the only way was to kill me.' She paused to take a couple of long, calming breaths. 'But then, of course, as a result of my stupid game, an innocent girl got killed in my place.'

I did my best to offer some comfort. 'Don't blame yourself,

Alice; last night was just a game. If Lucy's death turns out to have been murder, and at this point, we still don't know for sure, the fault lies with whoever did it, not you. You can't be held responsible for something like that. The inspector said she hoped to hear back from the pathologist this morning one way or another, and, if it turns out to be murder, she said she'd be coming back to interview everybody. I met her on Friday – she's a friend of a close friend of mine in the Florence murder squad – and she strikes me as a good, competent detective. When she comes here, I'd like the three of us to sit down together, and for you to spell out why you invited these particular guests and what shady secrets they might have in their past. She needs to have all the relevant information at her fingertips. You will be prepared to do that, won't you? Don't worry, I'll be with you all the way.'

She reached over and gave my hand a squeeze. 'Thanks, Dan, you're a sweetie, and of course I'll tell her the full story.' She released her grip on my hand and sat back, the forlorn expression back on her face again. 'I thought I was doing the right thing, getting everybody together and giving them a chance to hear my side of the story and hopefully, allowing them to apologise for what they did. Looking back on that decision now, I realise that it was naïve, to say the least. I should have known that tempers would run high but, even in my wildest nightmares, I never thought anybody would resort to murder.'

'If, indeed, it was murder. Let's see what the inspector tells us first.'

18

SUNDAY MORNING

It was eight-fifteen, and I'd just finished my breakfast when my phone bleeped to tell me that I'd received a text from Inspector Trevisan. It wasn't a long message.

> Definitely murder. Victim was poisoned. Please inform the others that I'll be coming over soon to interview everybody. I have an interpreter booked, but she won't be here until late morning. If you could help out, I'd be grateful. Thanks. Giulia.

For the sake of doing things by the book, I replied immediately.

> No problem, but are you sure you want me to help? Now that it's certain it was murder, I suppose I'm a suspect as well. Given that there are some very important people here, you're no doubt being scrutinised by your superiors. I wouldn't want to do anything that makes life difficult for you.

Her answer came back after less than one minute.

> Thanks, Dan, but I already thought of that and
> passed your name up the line. Would you believe
> the questore himself has spoken to his opposite
> number in Florence, and you've been given a
> glowing reference. All help gratefully received.

I glanced down at Oscar. 'It's not what you know, it's who you know.'

He was far more interested in the end of a croissant that I had given him, but he did at least wag his tail.

The only other guests sitting out under the pergola this morning were Greg Gupta and Carlos Rodriguez on one table, and Dirk Foster, all on his own at another. I swallowed the last of my coffee and went over to break the news to them that Lucy had been murdered. Gupta looked appalled, but Rodriguez just stared down into his coffee cup and gave no sign of even having heard what I'd said. When I went across to Foster, he, on the other hand, visibly paled when I gave him the news. If he was acting, he deserved every single award he'd ever won. He looked up at me with an expression of unbridled horror on his face.

'Murdered? She really was murdered? But how...?'

I decided to let the inspector answer this one when she got here, so I just shrugged my shoulders. 'At this stage, I'm afraid I don't know. Maybe drugs?'

'Surely not. We flew over from the States together and she told me she'd had a hiccup – that's what she called it – and she'd gone back on the drugs again for a few weeks, but that she was back off them again now. She sounded really committed this time.'

'This time? Had you spoken to her about this sort of thing before?'

He took his time before replying. 'Lucy and I had a thing together some years back. All right, so she's... she was a whole lot younger than me, but I really thought we might have had something. She'd been doing drugs before she met me, but I got her to stop, and she was doing really well before things fell apart between us.'

'Can I ask why things fell apart?'

Again, I had to wait for his answer, but when it finally arrived, it didn't really come as a major surprise. 'I screwed up. I was in London filming a movie with Carlos and I ended up in the wrong bed.' He looked up at me with what could have been genuine anguish in his eyes. 'What's wrong with me? I had this great girl back in the US and yet I still couldn't say no to some random woman I met at a party.' He hung his head. 'It's been the story of my life. I find somebody good and I screw it up. Thank God the media didn't get hold of it, but the news got back to Lucy all the same, and that was that. The relationship was over, and within days, she was back on the drugs again.' He reached out and caught hold of my arm. 'I screwed up her life and mine, and now she's dead. But who would want to kill her? She was so sweet...' His voice tailed off and I left him to his coffee and his regrets.

I found Alice in her study and I passed on the message from the inspector. I studied her face closely as the news that Lucy really had been murdered sank in. I saw her reach for a tissue but, before she could raise it to her face, tears of real grief came running down her cheeks. However good an actor she might have been, I couldn't see how these might be anything but signs of genuine sorrow. I sat quietly with her for a couple of minutes while Oscar at her side did his best to provide her with some much-needed support. Finally, she blew her nose and looked across the desk at me, her eyes still damp and bloodshot.

'Lucy's dead, and it's my fault. I was being selfish. I thought this weekend would be a good way of getting some kind of closure for me, but all it's done is to get a poor unfortunate creature killed. I don't know about you, Dan, but there's no doubt in my mind that the murderer's target was me. It should have been me lying there, not Lucy.' A lone tear rolled from one eye, and she dabbed at it with her tissue. 'How could I have been so stupid?'

'You weren't to know how extreme the reaction was going to be. Now, if you want to help Lucy, you need to concentrate on helping me and the police find out who did this.'

She nodded, and I decided the time was right to ask a few questions of my own before the police got here. 'When I was reading through your book last night, I found references to many of your guests this weekend, but I couldn't see any mention of Greg Gupta or Wilfred Baker. Were they just invited to fill out the cast of your murder mystery, or did they have a role in your past as well?'

She looked up from Oscar. 'Greg, no. He and Carlos are a couple, so where Carlos goes, he goes. I don't know what Greg sees in him. Greg's a nice guy, but Carlos is a pain in the ass.'

I gave her a gentle prompt. 'A pain in the ass who figures in your past, according to what I read last night. He said some uncomplimentary things about you, didn't he?'

She shrugged her shoulders. 'Like I say, he's an ass, but he's a dangerous ass.'

My ears pricked up. 'When you say "dangerous"?'

'Dangerous to my career. Louie, my agent, told me I'd been picked for the starring role in a movie, but then Carlos got chosen to direct it and he talked the producers out of casting me.' She looked across the desk at me and shook her head. 'That's what I mean when I say he's dangerous to my career.'

'But what would make him turn down a megastar like you?'

Her reply didn't come straight away. Finally, she looked up. 'He has a guilty conscience, and I imagine that seeing me reminds him of what he did, so he prefers to keep clear of me – and I've stayed out of his way as well up till now.'

'Can you tell me what he did? What gave him a guilty conscience?'

After another long pause, she explained. 'It was a long time ago, probably thirty years or so. I was in the running for an Oscar for my portrayal of Cleopatra, and my career was riding high. Everybody wanted a piece of me, and I was the toast of the town in LA. One night in June, I was invited to a party at Carlos's place – it's a ridiculous replica of a medieval castle just off Rodeo Drive. It was a wild night with people doing drugs and drinking to excess. At four minutes past midnight, one of the guests fell to his death from the top of the tower.'

'Four minutes past midnight? That's a very precise time. How can you be so sure?'

She looked up. 'Because I saw it happen, and the tower has a clock on it.'

'And what did happen?'

'The verdict was death by misadventure. The guy, a young actor called David Vernon, had been drinking heavily, and they said he must have slipped and fallen.'

I had a feeling I knew what was coming next, so I tried to ease her into it. 'But that's not what you saw?'

'I don't know what I saw. At least, I don't know how he came to fall, but what I did see was Carlos up there with him.'

'And you think he might have pushed the man over the edge?' This was serious. 'You think Carlos Rodriguez killed him?'

'I don't know. I don't see Carlos as a killer, but what struck me as suspicious, and what still strikes me as suspicious to this day, is that Carlos swore blind he was down in his cellar, looking for more wine, when it happened. Why would he lie about something as serious as that if he didn't have a guilty conscience?'

'And did Carlos see you looking up?'

'No question, eye contact. He saw me looking at him.'

'Have you ever spoken to him about that night?'

'I haven't spoken to anybody about that night. The police never questioned me and, looking back on it now, I suppose I didn't have the courage to come forward. After all, what could I say except that I'd seen Carlos up there? To be completely honest, I was doing cocaine in those days – recreationally, not mainlining – and I couldn't be totally sure about what I'd seen. I was afraid that the police might start investigating me, and the fallout could have been terminal for my career.' She shrugged her shoulders. 'So I said nothing.'

I filed this news away for further reference and queried the other name I hadn't found in her book. 'What about Freddie Baker? Does he get a mention? I couldn't see one.'

'He's there, all right.' She paused for thought for a few seconds. 'Take a look at the chapter headed "Falsehoods and Fabrications". You'll find him there.'

I decided to check that out before asking any more about her relationship with Baker, so I changed the subject slightly.

'You told me your intention was to sit down with each of the people who figure in your autobiography and see how they react. Have you had the chance to do that yet with any of them?'

'Not really. I had a quick word with Dirk yesterday lunchtime, but within seconds, we were arguing again.'

'It's clear from the book that you and Dirk Foster had a relationship twenty-five years ago, but that it ended acrimoniously.' Greg Gupta had already told me this, but I saw no point in involving him. 'I gather the two of you have hardly spoken since then. Can I ask why you invited him?'

'Like I said, I invited him because he's in the book, and because I wanted to give him the opportunity to apologise for what he did.' She looked me straight in the eye for a couple of seconds, and I read bitter anguish in them. 'He didn't only break my heart, Dan; he scarred me for life, mentally and emotionally.'

'You don't mention it in your book, but I read somewhere that you disappeared from circulation for a year after that. Something about a trip to India, if I remember right?'

She shook her head. 'You don't want to believe everything you read. If you want the honest truth, I went back to stay with my mum in Dorset. I needed to get away from Dirk and I needed to get away from Hollywood. I buried myself in the middle of the countryside and kept my head down.' She looked up at me and her eyes were bright with tears. 'I look back on that time of my life with mixed emotions. Mum was diagnosed with cancer while I was there, and I stayed with her till the end.'

'I'm sorry.' She was looking really down, so I did my best to cheer her up. 'But then you came back to Hollywood and picked up where you'd left off, and your career went ballistic. When your book comes out, I'm going to read it carefully, line by line. You describe some really happy times as well as some grim times. And, of course, you got married, didn't you?'

Her reaction to this was bittersweet. 'We got married in 2004. Andrew was a wonderful man. He was my rock, but then he was plucked away from me ten years ago, almost to the day.' She wiped her eyes again. 'A massive heart attack. One day, he was there; the next, he was gone.'

Any further nostalgia was interrupted by the sound of footsteps outside and I heard somebody tapping at the door, accompanied by a familiar voice. It was Mary. 'Miss Graceland, are you there? The police have arrived and they want to speak to everybody.'

I got up, opened the door, and let her in. When she saw Alice still wiping the tears away, she hurried over to her side of the desk and stood alongside her. 'Are you all right, Miss Graceland? Is there anything I can do to help?' She sounded genuinely concerned.

To my surprise and probably Mary's, Alice reached over, wrapped her arms around Mary's waist and buried her head against her side, sobbing quietly while Mary, clearly moved, stroked her boss's hair, doing her best to comfort her. At this point, Oscar was looking so concerned, I thought he was about to climb onto the desk to be close to them, so I thought it probably a good idea if he and I headed off and left the two of them alone.

* * *

Giulia Trevisan and Sergeant Scarpa were standing under the pergola. I went over and we shook hands. Formalities completed, I raised an inquisitive eyebrow in the inspector's direction. 'So the pathologist says she was poisoned; what sort of poison was it? Presumably, something quick-acting like arsenic?'

She shook her head. 'The pathologist's still trying to find out what it was. There were only very faint residual traces of heroin in the body, so it looks as though the victim really had been trying to kick the habit. Apparently, cause of death was myocardial infarction, heart attack, provoked by a very toxic poison, but one that's so uncommon that it may take all day or even several days to identify. In the meantime, though, what's clear is that the victim was poisoned so, unless she took it deliberately, that means murder. What we have to do now is to work out who did it.'

I nodded in agreement. 'I spent four hours last night reading the manuscript of Alice Graceland's autobiography. This raised a number of points. Let me tell you what I found.'

It took me a quarter of an hour to run through what I'd read overnight and heard from Alice and from Dirk Foster this morning. Both officers listened intently and took notes. When I finally reached the end of my account, Giulia reached into her pocket and handed me the cards Alice had distributed to the guests at the beginning of last night's murder mystery.

'Scarpa and I've been able to translate them more or less, but I'd like you to take a look.'

I glanced through them and what I saw perfectly matched what I'd read in the manuscript. Alice had simply translated the sins of the modern-day guests onto their Renaissance personae. Jack Sloane was a rapist, Desmond Norman a lecher, who had sought to take advantage of a young woman. Dirk Foster was a sex cheat and Carlos Rodriguez an offensive liar. I hadn't read about Freddie Baker in the manuscript yet, but seeing as he featured in the chapter 'Falsehoods and Fabrications', it seemed likely he would also turn out to be a liar. Maggie McBride was portrayed as a materialistic slut and – particularly of interest in this investigation – maybe even a poisoner. Only the sins of Alastair Groves, Alice's former agent, were unspecified. The words on his card were similar to what I'd read in her book: *You know what you did*. What, I wondered, had he done? Somehow, by refusing to specify what he'd done, this made it even worse.

I handed the cards back to Giulia and confirmed that they matched the contents of the manuscript. She took them from me, looked back down at her notebook, and summed up.

'Unless I've left somebody out, it looks as though the main suspects are Norman, Sloane, Foster, Groves, Rodriguez, McBride and probably Baker. That makes seven possibles.' She looked up at me. 'Right so far?'

This echoed my conclusions. 'Yes indeed, all of whom stood to face considerable embarrassment, and some possibly even complete humiliation and disgrace – or even prosecution – if the book were to get published as it is. Of course, they only had sight of the book after the murder had taken place, but the cards are quite unequivocal, so I think we have to assume that the killer is most probably the one with the guiltiest conscience, the one with the most to lose.'

'I agree, and, from what you've told us, Sloane could be facing a charge of rape, while Norman could be accused of a lesser, but still unpalatable, charge relating to his attempt to obtain sexual favours. Rodriguez could find himself being investigated in relation to the death at his party thirty years ago, although you and I both know that the evidence of a witness who admits to having taken cocaine would be trashed by any good defence lawyer. McBride faces humiliation if she really was sleeping around, looking for a billionaire, and if the poisoning comment on her card is correct, she could even be looking at a charge of murdering her husband. Foster more likely faces embarrassment or humiliation, and maybe Baker too, rather than anything more serious, but there has to be a question mark hanging over Groves, her former agent, until we find out exactly what he did – if anything. What do you think Alice Graceland meant when she wrote, "You know what you did"?'

I shrugged. 'I didn't have time to ask Alice when I was speaking to her just before you arrived. I must admit that I'm looking forward to hearing what she says about Groves and what he has to say for himself.'

The sergeant added a query of his own. 'What about other people here on the island? What about the wives and boyfriends of the main suspects, the staff here, the actors, or maybe even the owner herself? I wouldn't rule her out. At the moment, we're assuming the victim was murdered by mistake while the real target was Alice Graceland, but what if it's a clever double bluff, and the murder was committed by the owner, with or without the collaboration of her PA?'

I'd been thinking along these lines myself. 'It's a possibility, Sergeant, but I'm at a loss to know what motive Miss Graceland might have had for murdering the woman for whom she appears to have had considerable affection. But, you're right, we need to consider her, and I suppose we also need to bear in mind the staff members and actors just in case, along with the companions of the main suspects. Again, I can't see anything that links any of them with the murder, but who knows?'

The inspector closed her notebook with a snap and looked up. 'We need to start by interviewing the owner, followed by the principal suspects. Dan, if you're still available, will you help with interpreting, please?' She turned to the sergeant. 'Scarpa, find us a quiet room where we can conduct our interviews, and make sure everybody's up and available. We'll start with Alice Graceland.'

19

SUNDAY MORNING

The inspector, the sergeant, and I installed ourselves in the dining room on one side of the long table, with Oscar slumped on the floor at my feet. We had barely taken our places when there was a knock on the door and a constable ushered Alice inside. The inspector did the talking while I translated what she said, and what Alice said in response. Giulia started gently.

'You have a beautiful house, Miss Graceland. You've managed to convert what was a very run-down set of buildings into a comfortable, modern home without losing the authentic feel of the place. How long have you been living here?'

Alice looked weary but she replied readily enough. 'I bought the island two years ago, and the building work was finally finished just before Christmas. I've been here since then.'

'Writing your autobiography?'

'That's correct.'

'Mr Armstrong here has been telling me how the contents of the book and the cards you prepared for your murder mystery would appear to reveal that some of your guests have been carrying deep, dark secrets. I understand from him that your intention in inviting these people here was in the hope of receiving an apology from those who've behaved badly towards you. Is that correct?'

'Yes.' Alice's voice was expressionless, and I saw Oscar get up and trot around the table to position himself alongside her.

The inspector continued. 'What sort of apology were you expecting to get from the victim, Lucy O'Connell? What had she done to you?'

'Nothing at all. She was a friend, a good friend.' Alice was sounding more forceful now.

'So you're sorry she's dead?'

'I'm not just sorry, I'm broken-hearted.' Alice's voice faltered for a moment and tears appeared in her eyes once more. 'If you're asking me whether I had anything to do with her death, the answer is no, in the no uncertain terms. Like I say, she was a very close friend, and her death is a tragic loss.'

The inspector gave her a few moments to compose herself. 'I'm sorry I have to ask you these difficult questions, but I'm sure you're as keen as I am to get to the bottom of what happened. I have a number of questions for you about some of your guests. In particular—'

Before I could even start translating, the door was suddenly thrown open and one of the uniformed officers from last night appeared, looking flustered. The inspector shot him an exasperated glance.

'Yes, Piave, what is it?'

'I'm sorry to interrupt, ma'am, but you need to see this.'

'To see what? I'm in the middle of something here.'

'There's been another death.' The constable took a couple of quick breaths. 'I've been going around making sure that all the guests leave their rooms and collect on the terrace and when I got to room ten, I found the occupant inside stone dead.'

Giulia jumped to her feet and glanced at me. 'Dan, please would you apologise to Miss Graceland and tell her I've finished with her for now, but that we'll pick up this interview later?'

I repeated her message to Alice and then stood up as well and followed the inspector and the constable out of the door. Oscar seemed happy to stay with his new best friend, which was probably just as well if we were going into yet another crime scene, so I left him there with his nose on Alice's knees. For her part, she didn't say a word. She just sat there with an expression of intense grief on her face as she absently stroked Oscar's head.

As we hurried along the line of bedroom doors, I was trying to remember who had been the occupant of room ten, but it escaped me. I didn't have long to wait until I found out. Another officer was standing guard outside the open door, and I couldn't miss the bulky, yellow-clad shape lying on the bed. Jack Sloane, casting director and alleged rapist, was dead.

I followed the two police officers inside and stood by the door while Giulia checked that the victim was indeed dead and searched for any clues. I let my eyes roam around the room. The first thing I noticed was that the bed quite obviously hadn't been slept in, and the body was sprawled across it, face down. A few inches from his outstretched right hand was a copy of Alice Graceland's autobiography, also face down, and open. I glanced at the young officer beside me.

'Do you have a spare pair of gloves by any chance, Constable?'

He reached in his side pocket and handed me a pair of surgical gloves. Pulling them on, I went around to the other side of the bed and turned the manuscript over. I bent low and checked the text. It came as no surprise to see that this was the chapter in which Alice had recounted her ordeal at the hands of the *heavily overweight character over ten years older than me.* Of course, I reminded myself, this might be pure coincidence, but I doubted it. It would appear that Sloane had identified the reference to himself, so might this mean that he had decided to take his own life rather than face humiliation or worse?

Leaving the manuscript there, I walked back around to where Giulia was studying Sloane's bedside table. The light was still on and a half-empty bottle of single-malt whisky and a glass were resting there. I very carefully picked up the glass and studied it against the light, immediately spotting what looked like tiny specks of dust lying at the bottom of it. I set it back down again and, as I did so, the inspector caught my eye.

'You've seen that as well, have you, Dan? What's the betting he was poisoned with the same substance that killed the first victim? This is Sloane, isn't it? I didn't get a chance to speak to him yesterday but I remember you telling me he was drinking heavily. Whisky on the bedside table is a bit of a giveaway.'

I nodded. 'Jack Sloane, seventy-five years old, casting director and star-maker, and, from what I've seen of him this weekend, a serious alcoholic. If it really is poison in his glass, I wonder if he put it there or whether it was the work of somebody else.'

Giulia straightened up and stepped back from the bed. 'How's this for a scenario? Sloane finds out that Alice Graceland is about to reveal him to the world as a rapist, so he decides to take preemptive action. The card he receives at the murder mystery party convinces him of Graceland's intentions, so he poisons what he thinks is her drink or her fruit salad, but, because of the costume swap, Lucy O'Connell is killed instead. Back in his room, plagued by remorse, he uses the last of his poison to take his own life. What do you think? Case closed?'

Considering that similar thoughts had been going through my head, I nodded, but I wasn't convinced. 'It's definitely a possibility, but it throws up a number of questions. Presumably, this means that, when Sloane came to the island, he already had the poison in his possession. Apparently, rumours have been spreading around Hollywood that Alice Graceland has been writing a tell-all autobiography, so maybe he came with the express intention of committing murder. I've been wondering why such an obviously unhappy man with such clear antipathy towards his hostess should have accepted her invitation. Maybe he came to silence her.'

Constable Piave coughed politely. 'Could the poison be some medication that he was taking? Sleeping pills, maybe?'

The inspector answered. 'It's an interesting thought, Piave, but from the way Lucy O'Connell suddenly collapsed last night, I have a feeling we're looking for something much more quick-acting, but I'll get Forensics to check any medication they find here, as well as searching for the container that would have held the poison. But what do we think about the suicide theory? Do we think he took his own life?'

The constable looked unconvinced and, the more I thought about it, the less likely that scenario sounded to me. I did a bit of thinking out loud. 'Firstly, I don't see Sloane as the kind of person who would be racked with remorse. Aggressive and vindictive, almost certainly, but I don't see him as a candidate for suicide. If he was responsible for Lucy O'Connell's death, I could imagine him having another go at killing Alice, rather than trying to take his own life. He was probably worth a small fortune so if the book were to be published, he would easily have been able to afford to hire a top-notch legal team to fight any allegations in the courts. Another possibility is that somebody killed Lucy O'Connell and then deliberately murdered Sloane, staging the scene here in the hope that we would leap to the conclusion that Sloane killed Lucy and then himself – as you said, case closed.'

I pointed across to the manuscript on the bed. 'His copy of

Alice Graceland's book just happens to be open at the pages recounting her experiences at his hands. That strikes me as a bit too obvious. I think we could be looking for a completely ruthless murderer who killed the wrong person and is now trying to cover his or her back, or one who came here determined to kill Alice *and* Sloane.'

Giulia Trevisan nodded in agreement but, before she could reply, her phone started ringing. It was a short conversation, during which she said little more than 'thank you' a couple of times. When it ended, she looked across at the two of us with an expression of mystification on her face. 'That was the lab. They've identified the poison that killed Lucy O'Connell, and it's a new one on me. Have either of you ever heard of the suicide tree?' We both shook our heads, and she consulted her notebook. 'It's native to certain parts of India and its fruit is so highly poisonous that it can stop the heart in a matter of minutes, if not seconds, hence its popularity for suicide – or murder.'

A thought immediately flashed into my head. 'You said India. There's actually one guest here who's of Indian origin. Might Greg Gupta be more than just the innocent partner of Carlos Rodriguez? Have we been too quick to exclude him from our list of main suspects?'

Giulia looked up with interest. 'We both excluded Gupta because we couldn't see any possible motive he might have had for murdering either Lucy O'Connell or Alice Graceland but, of course, he might have done it to help his partner, whose dark secret of the man who fell to his death at Rodriguez's party was revealed to you by Alice Graceland. Maybe Gupta committed the murder, or both murders, in order to protect Carlos Rodriguez or, at the very least, he procured the poison so that Rodriguez could do the killing. Either way, I think this could be highly significant.'

She glanced at her watch and picked up her phone. 'It's gone nine-thirty. I need to get Forensics back over here and I need to brief my boss. As I told you, the *questore* himself is "taking a personal interest" in this case – no surprise there – so I've been instructed to report anything significant immediately. If you're happy to continue helping, Dan, why don't we pick up the interview with Alice Graceland at ten? That'll give you a bit of time to give Oscar a walk, and it'll give both of us time to do some serious thinking in the light of this latest death. See you at ten?'

'Of course.'

20

SUNDAY MORNING

As I walked across the grass towards Alice's study, I noticed that the door was open. Inside, I found Alice sitting on one of the sofas with a very happy Labrador sprawled across her lap, tongue hanging out, tail wagging. He deigned to look up when I came in but showed no sign of wanting to move ever again. She also looked up, her expression apprehensive.

'Diego has just looked in. Has there really been another murder, Dan? Who is it this time?'

'Jack Sloane.' I read surprise in her eyes, and even what might have been a hint of regret. For now, I didn't reveal that it had definitely been poison. When to reveal that information was up to the inspector so, for now, I kept it vague. 'It might be another murder or it might be natural causes; let's face it, the man was clearly drinking himself into an early grave. Alternatively, it might even have been suicide. The pathologist is on his way.' I decided that there was no harm in asking a question of my own. 'Are you surprised?'

It was a while before she replied. 'Yes, of course I'm surprised that anybody should die in my house, and to have two people dead in twelve hours is appalling. Am I surprised that it was Jack? Not really.' She looked up at me. 'Like you say, his drinking this weekend has been almost self-destructive, so if that was the cause, it doesn't come as a surprise, but I don't believe for a moment that he would have taken his own life.'

'Even though the allegations you level at him in your book could potentially even have led to criminal prosecution?'

She gave a dismissive wave of the hand. 'That wouldn't bother him. He would have bought his way out of trouble like he's always done.'

Clearly, her opinion of this most recent victim was the same as mine. 'And if it turns out that he was murdered? Would that surprise you?'

'Not really. Jack was one of the most hated people in Hollywood. What's that saying about great power bringing great responsibility? He certainly wielded an enormous amount of power and he would happily trample over anybody who stood in his way.' She ran a weary hand through her hair. 'I imagine you've read what happened to me at his hands, but I'm just the tip of the iceberg. I shudder to think how many young women have had their lives blighted by that bastard.' She paused to take a couple of deep breaths. 'I know they say you shouldn't speak ill of the dead but, in the words of Groucho Marx, in his case, I'll make an exception.'

I gave her a bit more time before I tried changing topic.

'Can you satisfy my curiosity about your former agent, Mr Groves? It's clear something bad happened to make you fire him, but you don't specify what it was. Would you feel like telling me? I'm sure the inspector would be interested to know as well.'

'Why, because she thinks Alastair might have wanted to kill me? That's not his style. The only killing he ever does is to people's reputations, and he's very, very good at that.'

'So what did he do that was so awful? Did he try to ruin your reputation after you sacked him?'

She glanced up and there was fire in her eyes. 'Of course he did, but he failed... and failed miserably.' She lapsed into silence for a full minute, but I didn't press her. When she finally started speaking again, her tone was deadpan and she kept her eyes trained on Oscar. 'What Alastair did really was awful, worse than Jack Sloane. He abused his position of trust and ruined the life of a seventeen-year-old girl.'

I waited for her to say more, but I waited in vain. In the end, I had to give her a little prompt. 'Was that seventeen-year-old girl you?' She shook her head without looking up, and I tried again. 'How exactly did he ruin this girl's life?' Although, given what I'd heard and read about Desmond Norman's and Jack Sloane's past behaviour, her answer about yet another member of the Hollywood aristocracy didn't come as a major surprise.

'He groomed her and then he defiled her.' Her voice was flat. 'He fed her promises of stardom and, all the while, he treated her as little more than his whore. She never fully recovered.' She finally raised her eyes from Oscar to me and, once again, I could see the tears sparkling there. 'Put simply, Dan, the man is an animal, and he behaved appallingly. When I found out what he'd done, I severed all ties with him and got myself a new agent with a bit more moral fibre.'

'But didn't the girl go to the authorities?'

She gave a snort of derision. 'In those days, she wouldn't have got anywhere, except for being blacklisted and booted out of Hollywood forever.'

'When you say, "in those days", what days are we talking about?'

'About twenty-five years ago.'

'You say he ruined her life. Where is she now?' I had a horrible feeling I knew who the girl was.

After another long wait, she finally shook her head, a note of resignation in her voice. 'She's dead.'

She buried her face in her tissue, and I decided to give her some privacy in her grief. I murmured, 'I'm sorry,' looked down at Oscar and uttered the magic word, 'Feel like carrying on with our walk?'

For a moment, I could see him looking uncertain. On the one hand, he could tell that his new best friend needed a bit of canine support, but at the same time, it was a *walk*, his favourite pastime after eating. Finally, he pulled himself to his feet, nuzzled her cheek once and followed me out of the door.

Outside, I breathed deeply, seeking to cleanse myself after what Alice had just told me. It was patently clear that she'd been talking about Lucy O'Connell. Beneath the glitz and glamour of Hollywood, the dark underbelly of the movie business – at least back in the not-too-distant past – had been laid bare. As Oscar and I walked around the garden, I reflected that this very definitely added the name of Alastair Groves to the list of Alice's guests with a lot to lose if the autobiography were to be published. I remembered Mary telling me that rumours had been circulating about Alice's intention of writing a no-holds-barred account, so this explained why people who hated her had accepted the invitation to come here, presumably hoping to find out what she intended to say about them. The problem the inspector and I now had was to work out which of them had come in the hope of redemption, and which had come determined to silence their accuser before it was too late.

I sat on the bench by the greenhouse, and my mind returned to the choice of poison. If this highly unusual toxin had its roots in India, could the only Indian guest here on the island be involved? I pulled out my phone and it didn't take long for me to discover that Greg Gupta and Carlos Rodriguez had been together for over ten years. In that time, they would no doubt have built up a strong bond of loyalty between them. Strong enough for Gupta to kill, to protect his partner? Or at least for him to supply his partner with the means to eliminate the woman whose memoir risked destroying Rodriguez's career?

I checked the time and saw that I had another ten minutes before I had agreed to meet up with the inspector again, so I searched the Internet for 'suicide tree'. Sure enough, I found numerous references to what was apparently a very beautiful tree of the oleander family, producing white flowers and fruit that gradually changed from green to red in the course of the season. For this reason, keen horticulturalists from as far afield as Australia and America were now using the tree for decorative purposes in spite of its fearsome reputation. Apparently, the poison lay in the seeds at the heart of the fruit, and even a tiny fraction of one of these could cause the death of a healthy adult in two or three hours. For somebody sickly, or with a compromised immune system, death could be almost instantaneous. I studied a photo of an Indian man in Kerala, India, standing alongside a bunch of the shiny, green fruit. The caption underneath gave the Latin name of the tree, *Cerbera odollam*, and a bell started ringing in my head.

Why was this name familiar to me?

It didn't take long for me to work it out. I scrolled back until I found the list of plants my new app had identified in Alice's greenhouse and, sure enough, there it was. I jumped to my feet and stared into the greenhouse. There, just inside the door and already almost touching the glass roof, was the tree. Even more interestingly, there were three or four green fruits hanging from its branches. Had I just found the murder weapon?

I retreated, ensuring that I closed the door firmly behind me. The last thing I wanted was for Oscar to mistake one of these lethal fruits for a ball. I stood there in silence for a minute or two, considering the implications of my find. Up till now, I'd been assuming that the poison had been brought to the island by the killer, but now, with it readily available here on the spot, things had changed. And, as far as our investigation was concerned, they hadn't changed for the better. This meant that anybody on the island with a knowledge of tropical plants – or simply with an app on their phone similar to mine – could have helped themselves to the fruit and crushed the seeds into a lethal powder.

The list of suspects had suddenly got longer, not shorter, and, like it or not, two names now had to be considered as serious contenders in that they both had had means and opportunity – although not necessarily motive. These two new suspects were, of course, Alice herself and Mary. As far as motive was concerned, the title of Alice's book said it all. What better way of getting payback against Jack Sloane than by killing him? But why kill Lucy O'Connell? From what Alice had just told me, she had felt very fond of Lucy, and I had believed her. It didn't make sense, unless Sloane's murder had been in revenge on the man she considered responsible for Lucy's death, but the chances of her somehow hitting upon the exact same highly unusual poison were so slim as to be not worth considering.

This, of course, left Mary, but what possible motive could a young woman with a doctorate in media studies have had for killing two people, both Hollywood icons in their own right? She had studied the movie world and she was no doubt more familiar with the darker side of Hollywood than an ordinary person, but what might she have discovered that could have driven her to commit two murders? I groaned and slumped back down onto the bench again.

Oscar returned from the fruitless chase of a big black and white butterfly and sat down beside me, no doubt aware that I was feeling frustrated. He almost immediately jumped to his feet again, tail wagging, and I looked around to see Inspector Trevisan approaching. She sat down on the bench alongside me, with Oscar stationed between the two of us.

'Well, I've spoken to the boss and he seems happy, so it's about time we started the interviews. Have you come up with anything in the meantime?'

I told her about my most recent conversation with Alice, and she listened intently before responding. 'And you say you believed her when she said she was very fond of Lucy O'Connell?' I nodded and she went on. 'So that probably rules her out as a suspect for the first murder, but it's clear that there was no love lost between her and Sloane. Might we be looking at two different killers? And, if so, our friend Signor Groves has leapt up the list of suspects with a lot to lose if the autobiography ever gets published after what he did to Lucy O'Connell.'

'You might well be right that we need to look for two different perpetrators and I agree about Groves, but there's something else I've just discovered, and it could be significant.' I went on to tell her about my discovery of the suicide tree growing only a few metres away from us, and she immediately realised the implications of this.

'That's all I need!' She gave a snort of frustration. 'So that means that anybody here on the island, including the staff and the actors, could have had access to the poison. What about Alice Graceland's PA, Mary Stevenson? She's been living here for six weeks. It's quite possible that she would have known about the poison plant. I think we'd better sit down and have a long talk to her as well.'

'What about the actors?'

'Scarpa is interviewing them as we speak. As you can imagine, they're pretty disgruntled that they've had to stay here overnight. They must have had an uncomfortable night. We've been checking their backgrounds, but we've found no dark secrets and nothing to link them with Lucy O'Connell, so it's unlikely that there's going to be any connection between any of them and the second victim either. It's the same with the staff. There's nothing that seems suspicious but, at least, we should be able to draw up a detailed picture of who was where when. The lab says that the poison was in the victim's fruit salad, and that was only served about ten or fifteen minutes before Lucy O'Connell's death, so hopefully, we should be able to find out if anybody was seen near the victim's table during that limited time period. Other people had the fruit salad with no ill effects, so the poison must have been slipped into hers alone.' She got to her feet. 'If you're ready, let's go and talk to the main suspects.'

21

SUNDAY MORNING

The interviews lasted most of the morning and they didn't throw up any great surprises. Alice repeated for the inspector's benefit what she'd told me about Groves and his abuse of Lucy O'Connell, and about the man falling to his death at Carlos Rodriguez's party. Mary told us about growing up in England, her university studies, particularly her interest in the film industry, and her plans for the future. By the end of her interview, I found it hard to believe that she could be our murderer, but I didn't write her off quite yet. She had certainly had the opportunity, but I was at a loss to come up with compelling motive for murder.

Desmond Norman looked stunned, but after two suspicious deaths in the space of a few hours, he had every right to look shocked. He freely admitted that he 'might have' propositioned Alice many years ago, but claimed that he didn't recall the specific conversation, and, of course, if he had done so, it would have been a joke. From his vagueness, even if we were charitable and bore in mind that this was an eighty-five-year-old man after all, the takeaway for both the inspector and for me was that in those days, such indecent propositions had been the norm rather than the exception, and there was a rotten taste in my mouth when the door closed behind him.

Dirk Foster repeated his confession of having cheated on Alice twenty-five years earlier and then doing the same to Lucy ten years ago, but he insisted that he'd never wished either of them any harm – and there certainly was no question of him wanting to kill either woman.

Carlos Rodriguez allowed himself to be reminded of the accident at his party all those years ago – 'What a terrible thing to happen!' – but he steadfastly repeated that he had been in the cellar at the time. When the inspector told him that this was contrary to what Alice claimed to have seen, he dismissed her testimony as, 'The ravings of a junkie; everybody knew she was doing cocaine.'

Greg Gupta, who was the next to be interviewed, came across as telling the truth when he claimed to have no motive whatsoever for killing either of the victims. When Giulia ask him about the suicide tree, he looked genuinely bewildered. If it was an act, it was a good one – and he was a scriptwriter, not an actor.

Freddie Baker was monosyllabic and totally unforthcoming but he, too, claimed to have been on good terms with both victims and he became decidedly prickly at what he described as the 'baseless insinuation' that he might have committed murder. His card for the murder mystery had only said that he was a fantasist and a liar but hadn't levelled any more serious allegations at him, so maybe he was telling the truth. He went on to refuse to say anything else until his lawyer was present. When asked, he informed us that his lawyer was in Los Angeles, so we would have to wait if we wanted to interview him further. He then started moaning at Giulia about being kept here and told her he would be contacting the American ambassador in Rome to complain in the strongest possible terms. Definitely not a happy bunny.

His companion, Antoinette Latour, appeared only too keen to help us with our inquiries but, fundamentally, it was clear that she knew very little about either of the victims. She told us that she was an artist and her relationship with Freddie Baker had started only a couple of months ago. From the impression I had already gained from her, I had the feeling the relationship wasn't going to last much longer.

This left us with Maggie McBride, who didn't mince her words when talking about her hostess. The 'sleeping around' comment in the book had gone down like a lead balloon, and the inspector had to struggle to tear her away from repeatedly bemoaning the scandalous – and of course completely unfounded – slur on her character and steer her onto the subject of the two deaths. McBride claimed to have liked both victims and scoffed at the idea that anybody might consider her a murderer. When Giulia suggested that the poison in Lucy's fruit salad might have been intended for Alice, McBride disclaimed all knowledge but, from her facial expression, it was clear it wouldn't have saddened her if the poisoner had hit the intended target. Given her already incandescent state, the inspector wisely avoided any mention of the husband-poisoning comment on her murder mystery card for now.

Her young partner, Rocco Gentile, was a New Yorker of Sicilian extraction who spoke a weird form of broken Sicilian dialect mixed with Americanisms, virtually incomprehensible to either the inspector or to me, so we conducted the interview in English. By the sound of it, he was a would-be actor and he told us proudly of a part he'd been offered in one of Maggie McBride's upcoming movies. I couldn't help reflecting that Hollywood's casting couches weren't just reserved for ambitious young women. As for the investigation, he told us that he and Maggie McBride had only recently got together and they didn't do a lot of talking; presumably they had other ways of passing the time. In consequence, he was unable to offer any help.

The last of the group to be seen was Alastair Groves, followed by his wife. Groves made an attempt to bluster his way out of the allegations of having taken advantage of seventeen-year-old Lucy, but he soon followed Freddie Baker's lead and refused to comment further about that without his lawyer being present. His wife, on the other hand, was clearly made of sterner stuff and she embarked on an aggressive defence of her husband – to whom she had been married at the time of the Lucy O'Connell saga. When she finally left the room, hurling accusations at everybody from Inspector Trevisan to the President of the Republic, and probably Oscar and me as well, I was glad to see the back of her. I found myself wondering which of the two I would have put my money on if Sandra Groves were ever to meet Maggie McBride in a boxing ring. Definitely two tough cookies.

Giulia and I finally emerged from the dining room at just after half-past eleven and went over to the bench by the greenhouse, where we sat down and enjoyed a bit of fresh air while Oscar went off to water the plants. She turned towards me and raised an eyebrow.

'Well, *Commissario*, who's your money on?'

'If you'd asked me at midnight last night who was most likely to have tried to murder Alice, I would have said Jack Sloane without a doubt. He had a lot to lose and he certainly struck me as a tough enough character to be able to carry out a simple poisoning. Now that he's dead, I suppose the question we have to ask ourselves is whether we think he was responsible for last night's death and then took his own life, or whether we're looking for a different person who came here to kill him and Alice, or who killed Lucy and then callously killed Sloane to try to incriminate him for that murder.'

She nodded in agreement. 'I think we're looking for one murderer, not two. My feeling is that whoever killed Lucy O'Connell also killed Jack Sloane.'

'I agree with you, not least because of the unusual poison being used in both cases. I'm convinced that Lucy wasn't the original target last night. I definitely believe that the poison was intended for Alice Graceland. Is that what you think?'

'I do. We have any number of suspects who stood to lose a lot in prestige, or possibly even face serious legal complications, if that book ever got published. Any one of them would have been delighted to see Alice Graceland dead. What I've been trying to work out is whether one of them might have wanted to kill her *and* Sloane, but I'm struggling to find a motive for both.'

I did a bit of thinking. 'One thing I'm sure you've noticed is that the bedroom doors don't have locks. I suppose that's because Alice wanted to keep the feel of a private house, rather than a hotel. This means that anybody could have gained access to Sloane's room last night to spike his drink. On that basis, everybody on the island had opportunity and, with a poisonous plant only a few feet away, they would also have had means. The poisoner most probably sneaked over to Sloane's room and spiked his drink on Saturday night while the party was taking place. As you say, what we need to discover is the possible motive anybody might have had for wanting both Alice – or maybe Lucy – and Sloane dead.' Another thought crossed my mind. 'I can't remember anybody leaving the party except for one. When Alice handed out the cards, Dirk Foster stormed off and didn't return until you arrived – but I'm lost for a motive for him to have poisoned Sloane.'

Giulia's phone bleeped and she glanced at it. 'The interpreter's arrived, so you're in the clear from now on, Dan. Thanks a lot for all your help. I'm going to organise a fingertip search of all the rooms, just in case we get lucky and find some trace of the poison.' She waved vaguely at the surrounding walls. 'Although it would be the easiest thing in the world to climb up onto the battlements and drop any incriminating evidence in the lagoon. Scarpa should have finished interviewing the staff and actors by now and, unless he's unearthed any surprises, I'm going to let the actors leave the island with strict instructions not to go to the media. Hopefully, Scarpa should also have been able to draw up a plan of who was where at the time of Lucy O'Connell's murder. The killer needed to get close enough to her table to poison only *her* fruit salad.' She gave me a wry smile. 'In an ideal world, we would find that only one or two people went near her, but, as you and I both know, we don't live in an ideal world.'

After she'd gone off, I climbed up onto the battlements and did a full circuit of the island, looking inwards as well as outwards. I found no trace of a container that might have held the poison or anything compromising – like a pair of discarded gloves. All I spotted was a very smart-looking speedboat moored up in front of Diego's launch on the jetty. Presumably this was Freddie Baker's chosen means of transport. Once again, I marvelled at a city where, instead of renting a car, you rented a boat to get around. Venice certainly is a unique place.

Back in my room, I picked up Alice's book and looked up the chapter headed 'Falsehoods and Fabrications' for mention of Freddie Baker, but I found little of interest apart from the confirmation of what Antoinette had told me and what Alice had written on his card. According to Alice's book, Freddie Baker had a reputation as a fantasist who invented facts to suit his purposes, a purveyor of fake news. He was apparently not above writing his own glowing reviews and exaggerating his own success. I remembered what he'd told Jack Sloane yesterday lunchtime and I managed to find a website listing the biggest-grossing movies of the past years. I had to scroll a long way down last year's list to find *Dancing and Singing*, the musical about which Sloane had been so scathing, and which Baker had claimed to have grossed half a billion dollars. The figure given on the list – updated barely a month ago – was just over two hundred million dollars – still a lot of money, but nowhere near half a billion. However, none of this gave me any indication of why he might have come here determined to murder two people.

As I looked around the interior of the fortress, I spotted Diego and his son setting up their drinks stall under the pergola. It wasn't noon yet, but I needed a refreshing drink.

I glanced down at Oscar, who was casually scratching his ear with his hind leg. 'Fancy a beer?'

I don't give him beer, but he knows that it normally comes with crisps or salted biscuits, so he abandoned his toilette and headed for the nearest staircase, tail wagging.

22

SUNDAY LATE MORNING

Diego saw me coming and he was already pulling out my replica Renaissance mug and two bottles of ice-cold beer by the time I got to him. He filled the mug to the top and handed it over to me.

'Busy morning?'

I took a big mouthful of beer and let it slide slowly down my throat. It was another boiling-hot day and the refreshment was very welcome. Diego pointed downwards and I saw that he had even prepared a bowl of water for Oscar, so the two of us quenched our thirst together before I gave my answer.

'I've been acting as interpreter while the inspector has been questioning the guests. She strikes me as a very competent officer.'

'And is she getting anywhere with the investigation?' I saw him take a careful look around but, for the moment, we were alone. 'Do you really think it was one of this lot?' He waved in the general direction of the guest bedrooms.

There was no point in dissimulation. 'It looks that way.'

'So who do you think did it?'

I decided to turn the tables on him. 'I'm still trying to work that out. Do you have any theories?'

He leant towards me and lowered his voice. 'You know what I think? I think whoever killed that poor woman last night was actually trying to kill Miss Graceland.'

'You could well be right, but why?'

Still keeping his voice low, he continued. 'I've been talking to Mary this morning, and she's been telling me some of the stuff that Miss Graceland says in her autobiography. By the sound of it, there are some really rotten apples here. Any one of them could have done it out of spite, or to shut her up.'

'You could be right about that as well. Any thoughts on who the perpetrator or perpetrators might be?'

He shook his head but he hadn't finished yet. 'I don't know enough about them but, in my experience, it's got to either be about sex or money.'

I grinned at him. 'Have you ever thought about becoming a detective, Diego? That sounds like a very profound statement.'

At that moment, the door behind him opened and Mary came out. While Diego was pouring her what looked like a shot of brandy, I reflected on what he'd just said. Certainly sex had raised its head on numerous occasions during the questionable careers of a number of the guests, but what about money? I was assuming that they all had more than enough, but what I consider to be enough money and what Hollywood moguls consider enough are two different things entirely. Who was likely to gain by the deaths of Alice and Sloane? I decided that I would spend time this afternoon trawling the Internet in the hope of discovering the financial circumstances of all the guests.

Mary came over to me and received a warm welcome from Oscar. She was looking very emotional, and, from what I could see, she'd recently been crying. She took a mouthful of her brandy and grimaced. I seized on that as an intro.

'Don't like the cognac?'

She shuddered. 'I never normally drink anything like this, but I felt I needed something.' She sounded quite breathless, and I was genuinely concerned for her.

'Are you feeling all right? Come and sit down.' I led her over to a nearby table. Oscar, already on the case, immediately sat down alongside her and put a reassuring paw on her thigh. She reached down to catch hold of it, and I tried to offer some support of my own. 'I'm afraid murder's never pretty, and two in the space of a few hours is bound to be upsetting.'

Her response came as a surprise. 'It's not the murders.' She stopped and corrected herself. 'I mean, yes, of course they're horrific, but it's not that. I've been talking to Miss Graceland, and she's told me something that I'm finding really hard to process.'

'Bad news?'

'No, not bad, definitely not bad. Just mind-blowing.'

I sat back and waited, deliberately giving her time to marshal her thoughts. Finally, she looked up from Oscar straight at me, her eyes wide with disbelief. 'She's just told me that I'm her daughter.'

'Her daughter?'

My immediate reaction was one of astonishment, but then in its wake came the realisation that something that had been quietly ticking away in the back of my mind had been revealed as fact, not conjecture. Suddenly, Alice's alleged freak-out and disappearance for a whole year after the break-up with Dirk Foster a quarter of a century ago was explained – but hadn't Mary told me her parents had been an Italian mother and an English father? Unless...? I tried to be as diplomatic as possible.

'But your mum and dad? You were brought up in England, weren't you?'

I had to wait quite a while before Mary replied, her voice hoarse with emotion. 'My mum and dad – and I always thought of them as my mum and dad – adopted me as a teeny tiny baby. I was only six days old, and they looked after me and loved me all my life.' Tears were now running down her cheeks, but she let them run. 'When I was eighteen, my mum broke the news to me that I'd been adopted and she offered to show me my birth certificate, but I told her I didn't want to know. As far as I was concerned, *she* was my mum, not some woman who'd abandoned me as a newborn baby.' She stopped to take another sip of the cognac, but she hastily put the glass down again in disgust and wiped her hand across her mouth. 'Dad died three years ago, and my mum died this Easter, and I thought that was it. I thought I was all alone in the world, and now this...'

At this point, Oscar took matters into his own paws, stood up on his hind legs and reached up to kiss her cheek – well, actually more of a slobbery lick. This simple act of affection was all it needed, and floods of tears came pouring out in earnest. I went across to where Diego was looking most concerned and asked for a glass of water. As he handed it to me, I gave him a little smile and told him not to worry, Mary was going to be okay. I picked up a handful of paper napkins and went back over to her, glad that none of the guests had decided to put in an appearance yet. I pressed the napkins into Mary's hands, set the water down in front of her and waited. It took several minutes, but she finally managed to regain a semblance of control, wiped her eyes and face and took a big mouthful of water.

I looked across and gave her a reassuring smile. 'Feeling a bit better?' She gave me a little nod of the head and a hint of a smile so I went on. 'What about Miss Graceland? How's she handling this?'

Mary wiped a napkin across her face again. 'She's inside, crying her eyes out. She broke the news to me half an hour ago, maybe an hour ago, and she's been crying ever since.' She sniffed and wiped her face again. 'And so have I.' She looked across the table at me. 'I don't think either of us really know why we're crying. I'm just so confused.'

I could well believe it. I glanced at her as she returned her attention to Oscar, catching his head between both her hands and kissing him on the nose. I decided that this wasn't the moment to tell her that he used that nose for all sorts of far less hygienic activities and did my best to offer moral support.

'Of course you're confused, anybody would be. Just give it time, and let it sink in.'

I wondered whether she had already worked out what this meant as far as her real father was concerned. By the sound of it, she wasn't the only one who was going to get a shock. I found myself wondering how Dirk Foster would handle this bombshell. My thoughts shifted to Alice, and I wondered why she had decided to seek out the baby she'd given up all those years ago. The significance of her words to me about Dirk Foster – 'He didn't only break my heart; he scarred me for life, mentally and emotionally' – was now revealed. Presumably, she had offered Mary a job as a means of getting her close, but I wondered why she'd taken six weeks to break the news to her and why she'd chosen today of all days for such an explosive revelation. Feelings and emotions have never been my strong points – ask my ex-wife or Anna – but I felt sure that in this case, there was one course of action that Mary really should be following. I leant towards her.

'Miss Graceland... your mother is in there on her own, crying. You're out here, crying. Don't you think it might be better if you went back to her? You both have a lot to talk about, and the sooner you get started, the better.'

Mary nodded slowly, gently lifted Oscar's paws off her lap and stood up. She then came around to my side of the table and kissed me on the cheek. 'Thank you, Dan. You're right.' And she went back over to the house and disappeared inside.

Diego was still looking at me with an expression of considerable curiosity on his face, but I decided that it would be down to Alice and Mary to tell him what had just transpired. I gave him a little wave, picked up my mug of beer and went back to my room, where I opened my laptop and set about investigating the financial status of the various guests.

Without the resources of the police behind me, I was unable to access bank details of the guests, and most of my information had to come from reading press releases and articles in the various industry journals. What emerged was that I'd been right in my supposition that all of them – including Alice – were doing very well indeed, except for one. As his girlfriend had hinted, Freddie Baker needed money – not pocket money, but serious cash.

He had a magnificent-looking villa in Beverly Hills and clearly more than enough money to allow him to fly across the world and rent what was probably a very expensive speedboat here in Venice, but what he needed was hefty financial backing to allow him to carry on making his movies. Probably unwisely, he had set up his own production company earlier this year and rumours were swirling around that it was close to insolvency. It was pretty clear that his prickly personality, as described by Antoinette, and as witnessed by Giulia and me, had alienated any number of possible financiers and he was apparently floundering, desperately seeking the many millions needed to make his new movie. In particular, it appeared that he was being blocked by a shadowy, but very influential, organisation referred to in several of the more sensationalist trade papers as 'the Bloc'. As far as I could tell, this was a cartel of media millionaires and billionaires, without whose backing it was almost impossible for an independent filmmaker to get the necessary money to go ahead.

The problem from my point of view was that, however strapped for cash Baker's company might be, I couldn't see how this could have produced a motive for murder. Maybe Diego's other suggestion was the right one, and the origin of the murders was sex after all. The damage that Alice's autobiography could do to the reputations of some very powerful people had brought one of them here intent of silencing her for good.

23

SUNDAY LUNCHTIME

The sound of the lunch gong summoned me before I could dig any deeper into the mysterious Bloc organisation, and a glance at my watch told me that it was almost one o'clock. In case I might have had any thoughts of carrying on working and turning up late for lunch, Oscar walked over to his spotlessly clean food bowl and stuck his nose right into it before glancing around at me and uttering a plaintive yelp. I might be prepared to be late for lunch, but he certainly wasn't. I took the hint, abandoned my online research and got up. I filled his bowl and, by the time I had washed my hands, he had hoovered it all up and was slurping up a bellyful of water to wash it down. He really doesn't take his time and savour his food.

We went outside and headed for the pergola, where lunch was being served. As we walked, it occurred to me that I might be able to find out more about the mysterious Bloc by talking to some of the guests over lunch – although I would have to pick my interviewees carefully.

Lunch today was roast beef in a thick, red-wine-based sauce. As an alternative, Diego was busy grilling fresh fillets of fish, sardines, skewers of prawns, squid rings and octopus. Along with these were grilled peppers, slices of cauliflower and even halves of red lettuce, sprinkled with olive oil and cooked on the barbecue. It all looked and smelt amazing.

I looked around and did a rough count-up. Most of the guests had assembled – unsurprisingly, none of them deciding to come and eat with me after my presence alongside the inspector earlier – but there were a few notable absences. I spotted Antoinette, but there was no sign of Freddie Baker. Alastair Groves was here, but not his wife, and the most significant absentees were Alice, Mary and Dirk Foster. I hoped this meant that Foster was sitting down with mother and daughter, digesting and discussing the momentous news.

Anna had prepared some excellent roast beef for my mum and dad last weekend so, seeing as we were not only at the seaside but immersed in it, I decided to go for a plate of assorted grilled fish. Along with this, Valentina gave me a slice of toasted bread rubbed with garlic and drizzled with olive oil and a couple of slices of grilled cauliflower and grilled red lettuce. Grilled lettuce and cauliflower were something new to me, but I accepted gratefully, keen to try something out of the ordinary.

I saw the inspector and the sergeant sitting at a table at the far end of the pergola, and when Giulia caught my eye, she waved to me to come over. I waved back but stopped off first for a quick word with Antoinette before her boyfriend put in an appearance.

'Hi, Antoinette, can I ask you something? Have you ever heard of something called the Bloc?'

She gave a weary sigh. 'That's just about the only thing Freddie ever talks about. According to him, they're out to get him. Worse than the Mafia, he calls them.'

'And who is "them"? Do they have names, these people?'

'It's all very secret, as far as I can tell. I've no idea how many of them there are or who they are but, according to something Freddie said this morning, the leader was Jack Sloane.'

'Sloane?' I felt a surge of excitement. Surely this had to be more than a coincidence. 'I didn't think Sloane was a financier. Wasn't he a casting director, a talent scout?'

She nodded. 'A very *rich* talent scout. According to Freddie, he's one of the richest men in Hollywood. His name almost never appears in the credits, but he's been executive producer of all manner of movies, most of them making him an awful lot of money.'

I thanked her for the information and made my way across to the inspector and the sergeant. Sergeant Scarpa pushed out a chair for me and I sat down. Oscar wandered around to say hello to the two of them, while Giulia brought me up to date.

'Between us, we've interviewed everybody who was at the party last night and we've managed to draw up a plan of exactly who was where when the first murder took place. The bad news is that everybody was supposed to swap tables just before dessert was served, so almost anybody could have gone past the table where Lucy O'Connell was killed in the fifteen minutes between the fruit salad being brought out and the victim's death. Forensics have tested what was left of the fruit salad in the main serving bowl and there's no trace of the poison, so somebody must have got close enough to the victim's table to be able to drop the poison into her dish. Ironically, the only guest who didn't go near the victim's table was Jack Sloane. Nobody can recall him moving out of the seat he occupied from the very start of the evening, and people who sat with him at various times during the meal report that he had no interest in the mystery whatsoever and just sat there drinking and silently fuming.'

I had been listening, but my mind was still processing the possible significance of what Antoinette had just told me. Still, when Giulia stopped talking, I managed to summon up a bit of interest. 'At least it removes one possible line of conjecture. On that basis, it seems quite clear that Sloane almost certainly can't have murdered Lucy O'Connell, so the scenario of him committing murder and then taking his own life would appear to be a non-starter.'

The two officers nodded, and I took a few bites of my lunch. In particular, the grilled red lettuce turned out to be unexpectedly excellent, but my mind was on the case rather than the food. Through a mouthful of fish, I asked another question.

'What about people slipping away from the party to lace Jack Sloane's whisky with poison?'

The sergeant shook his head. 'Anybody or nobody. With all the table changing, it would have been easy for anybody to have gone off for a few minutes without any of the others noticing. Mind you, there was one person who definitely left for about ten minutes. Mary Stevenson went into all the rooms, delivering copies of the book. She, more than anybody else, had every opportunity to add the poison to the whisky.' He gave me a look that said quite clearly that he considered her to be a prime suspect.

I had been expecting something inconclusive so I was disappointed, but not surprised, that the only definite absentee had been Mary, but I didn't share the sergeant's opinion of her as a killer. I was just about to tell them about Freddie Baker and the mysterious Bloc organisation when Giulia gave me a searching look and I realised that I'd been right when I'd thought that she didn't miss much.

'What's on your mind, Dan? I can almost hear your brain churning. Have you discovered something?'

I gave her a smile. 'You're dead right. I'm still trying to get my head around what I've learned over the last few minutes. Does the name "the Bloc" mean anything to you?'

They both shook their heads, and I recounted what I'd read online and what Antoinette had just told me. As I did so, I saw her exchange glances with the sergeant. As soon as I'd finished, she delivered judgement.

'That's fascinating. From what Antoinette Latour has told you about Freddie Baker being short of cash and convinced that he was the victim of a deliberate campaign by the mysterious cartel, I think we should seriously consider him for the murder of Jack Sloane, but I still can't see any reason why he would want to kill either Lucy or Alice.'

I nodded in agreement. 'My thoughts exactly. We must be missing something. How did the search of the guests' rooms go?'

Sergeant Scarpa answered. 'Nothing suspicious. As well as searching the bedrooms, Forensics have been poking around the whole complex, including the gardens, but without seeing anything untoward. Whoever it was who killed the first or even both victims, we're going to struggle to prove it.'

Giulia looked similarly pessimistic. 'I'll get onto my people back at the station and ask them to investigate this Bloc organisation, but I'm not going to hold my breath for an immediate breakthrough. As Scarpa says, we're struggling, and I'm conscious that these people – important people with friends in high places – are expecting to be able to leave tomorrow at the latest. I've already had a number of them asking for permission to go today. I've said no, and it didn't go down well.'

I sat there and thought about it as I picked at my food. To my shame be it said, I barely tasted what was yet another excellent meal and I could almost feel the disapproval emanating from my ever-hungry Labrador. I handed him down a couple of prawn heads – and they disappeared in a flash – while I did a bit more thinking out loud.

'But Freddie Baker isn't the only one. It wouldn't surprise me if Sandra Groves turned out to be the person who tried to murder Alice. She struck me as a particularly tough character. Her husband potentially has a lot to lose if the book comes out, so she had a strong motive to silence Alice – or even Lucy, who is, after all, the only witness to what happened when she was an abused teenager. Carlos Rodriguez – maybe aided and abetted by Greg Gupta – had motive to kill Alice, because she saw what happened at his party all those years ago, but why wait so long to silence her? Maggie McBride is clearly furious with Alice after what was in the book, but surely hurt pride isn't normally enough to make people resort to murder. But even if it was one of them, why kill Sloane as well?' I looked up from my plate of rapidly cooling food. 'Maybe we *are* looking at two different perpetrators after all.'

The sergeant's gloomy expression darkened. 'And we don't have a shred of proof against any of them.'

I nodded in agreement. 'Then there's the question of the poison. I doubt whether any of the guests would have recognised the suicide tree here in the greenhouse, so my feeling is that the killer must have brought the poison with them.'

'Unless the killer was Graceland herself or her PA, Mary Stevenson.' The sergeant wasn't giving up on his original theory.

I shared another grilled prawn with Oscar. 'Anything's possible, Sergeant, but there's been an interesting development on that front in the last few minutes.' I went on to tell them what Mary had just told me about her parentage and both officers looked as surprised as I had originally felt.

The inspector was the first to react, echoing my own thoughts. 'I wonder why Alice Graceland chose today, of all days, to break the news to her daughter?' She glanced around, but there was nobody near enough to hear. 'Assuming that it did come as news to Mary Stevenson. Might she have been play-acting, Dan? Might the two of them be working together to murder their guests?'

'I seriously doubt it. Mary looked totally convincing to me. I may be completely wrong – it wouldn't be the first time – but I can't see what possible reason either of them might have had for killing Lucy O'Connell – Sloane, maybe, but surely not O'Connell. I believed Alice when she said she loved Lucy dearly. As for why Alice chose today to give Mary the news, I'm only guessing, but I wonder whether she deliberately planned to tell Mary when Dirk Foster, the father, was here as well.' I tasted a piece of the grilled cauliflower, now cold, and decided that I wouldn't be in a hurry to try this again on my own barbecue back home. I handed a piece down to Oscar for his opinion and, most unusually for him, he took it suspiciously, held it in his mouth for a couple of seconds and then deposited it on the ground with an affronted expression on his face.

While I was still registering the fact that I had at last found a food that even my omnivorous dog wasn't prepared to eat, the inspector took a drink of water and sat back. 'As you so rightly say, Scarpa, we are desperately short of proof. To make matters worse, I agree that we might have to start looking for two different killers, rather than just the one, simply because it seems impossible to find any of the guests with a motive for murdering both. I'm going back to the office to see how they're getting on checking the backgrounds of everybody here and to look into this Bloc cartel, but I have a feeling my superiors aren't going to be too happy.' She sighed and stood up. 'You never know, maybe we'll have a stroke of luck. We certainly need it.'

24

SUNDAY AFTERNOON

After giving Oscar a walk around the garden, I went back to my room to resume my online investigation. There had been no sign of Alice, Mary or Dirk Foster, and I hoped this meant that they'd been able to sit and discuss things amicably. Before opening my laptop, I called Anna to tell her what had been happening, and I heard her groan.

'What is it about you, Dan? Everywhere you go, murder seems to follow you. So who's the murderer this time? Don't tell me you haven't solved the case by now?'

I decided it would take far too long to run through all the suspects so I just muttered something about needing a bit of time and changed the subject to her holiday in the mountains. She told me all about the long walk she'd had this morning and how much Oscar would have enjoyed being there and then she reminded me of my obligations. 'Have you phoned your mum? She was complaining that you're awful at staying in touch, so why not surprise her with a phone call?'

I can recognise a direct order when I hear it, so when my call to Anna finished, I obediently rang my parents. Mum answered the phone and immediately told me off.

'Daniel, honestly, you phone at the most inconvenient times. I've just put the roast on the table, and your father's carving it as I speak. Is something wrong?'

I adopted my humblest tone. 'Nothing's wrong, Mum, and I'm sorry about the timing. I forgot the UK's an hour behind Italy. I just wanted to ring and tell you that I'm okay and to see how you two are doing.'

Just like Giulia Trevisan, my mum doesn't miss much. 'Anna put you up to it, didn't she? I bet she told you to call.' I mumbled something in reply, and she took pity on me. 'Well, I'm pleased to say we're both fine, and it's good of you to call. Now I'm going to hand you to your father while I go and get the gravy.'

A couple of seconds later, I heard my father's voice. 'Hello, Dan, you okay?' He never was a great conversationalist, but then neither am I.

'Hi, Dad.' There was silence for a couple of seconds before, desperate for something to say, all I could think of was the case. 'I'm here in Venice and two people, Hollywood people, have been murdered. It's a complex case, and I'm a bit stumped.'

This brought an immediate reply. He wasn't the father of the boy in the Sherlock Holmes Club for nothing. 'Presumably, it was the same killer in both cases?'

'That's pretty much the conclusion I've come to, but I'm struggling to find motive for both murders.'

'Same MO?' I had a feeling he'd been watching more of his beloved murder mysteries on TV. He certainly sounded as if he had picked up the jargon. I confirmed that they had indeed both been killed in the same way and he carried on. 'Were the victims male or female?'

'One of each.'

'Were they romantically involved with each other?'

'No.' I waited for him to give me his verdict. I was actually quite interested to hear what he would say. I needed all the help I could get with this case.

'Then it has to be about money. Follow the money... Hang on, your mother's telling me to hang up.' And that was that.

My father's words echoing in my ears, I opened the laptop and set about getting to the bottom of whether the mysterious Bloc actually existed and, if so, doing my best to find the names of any of the shadowy characters involved with it. After at least half an hour, I hadn't got much further, but then one line in an article in one of the lesser-known showbiz journals caught my eye.

Although membership of the Bloc is a closely guarded secret,
it has been reported that it is made up not just of financiers,
but also movie professionals and well-known actors.

Well-known actors. I sat there and stared at the words for a few seconds. Here I was on an island belonging to one of the best-known, and no doubt wealthiest, actors in the world. What if Alice were a member of the Bloc? Suddenly, I had a feeling I might have discovered the motive a single perpetrator might have had for killing both Sloane and Alice.

Was Freddie Baker the murderer?

Had he come here to kill the two members of the cartel that he saw as the obstacle to his success? This, of course, would give him motive, he certainly would have had the opportunity, but what about the means to commit two murders? Was it possible that he'd chanced upon the suicide tree here in the greenhouse, or had he come prepared?

I checked back onto some of the websites I'd seen mentioning him and, in particular, his luxurious villa in the mock-Renaissance style. Remembering what I'd read in the article about the suicide tree now being used by garden designers because of its aesthetic appearance, I scanned the gardens surrounding his house closely. It didn't take long. Standing in the middle of a luxuriant lawn – no doubt watered by a sprinkler system – was a tall, statuesque tree, covered in white blossoms. Without question, here it was – *Cerbera odollam,* the suicide tree.

I slammed the laptop shut and jumped to my feet, rousing Oscar from dreams of prawn heads and Alice Graceland. As I headed for the door, I turned to call him.

'Come on, dog, we're going to see your girlfriend.'

It was baking hot outside and many of the guests had retired to their air-conditioned rooms, but not all of them. I heard splashing coming from the pool and spotted two people sitting against the perimeter walls in the shade on the far side of the island, deep in conversation. I was interested to see that these were Dirk Foster and Mary and I left them alone; they had a lot to talk about. Instead, I hurried across to Alice's study and tapped on the door. I rather expected her to be having a siesta, but I was delighted to hear a voice from inside telling me to come in. I opened the door, stepped inside, and made sure I closed it firmly behind me.

Alice was reclining on one of the sofas and I had the suspicion that I had indeed interrupted her snooze, but this was potentially far more important and urgent than an afternoon nap. She waved me over, and the weary expression on her face was replaced with a smile as Oscar climbed straight onto the sofa and stretched out across her lap, his tail sweeping the leather as he did so. She seemed only too happy to let him climb on the furniture, so I let him be and sat down opposite her. I got straight to the point.

'Hi, Alice, I'm sorry if I disturbed you, but there's something really urgent I need to ask you. Would I be right in thinking that you're involved with something called the Bloc?'

The cosy expression on her face suddenly changed to a much more guarded one. 'Who told you that, Dan?'

'Nobody, Alice, it's just an idea that came to me. Listen, I know this is all top secret and I guarantee you that anything you say will be strictly between the two of us and the inspector, but it could be the key to solving both murders. Most particularly, if you *are* involved with the Bloc, I think that confirms that Lucy's murderer was indeed aiming for you rather than her last night, and your life could still be in danger.'

I sat back expectantly, mentally crossing my fingers in hope. She didn't answer immediately but, when she did, things started to become clear in my head.

'I trust you, Dan, and so I'm going to tell you. Yes, I have been involved with the Bloc for a few years now, although I made up my mind to step back from any further involvement ever since Jack Sloane took over at the head a month ago.' She caught my eye. 'It's been bad enough seeing him in Zoom meetings without having to meet him face to face. Of course, now that he's dead, I might have to review that decision, but I've got far too much going on in my head at the moment to even begin to think of that. What made you ask?'

There was no subtle way of saying this, so I just went for it. 'I believe the person who murdered Lucy, thinking it was you, and then murdered Jack Sloane, was Freddie Baker.'

She looked genuinely stunned and, before she could voice her scepticism, I carried on. 'Baker has his own production company, and the word on the street is that it's in serious financial difficulty. I've been talking to Antoinette, and she tells me he's convinced himself that the Bloc cartel has, in his words, got it in for him. Now, I don't know whether that's right or not, but it seems to me that he came here determined to take radical action against two people that he knew to be part of the Bloc.'

'You really think Freddie came here to kill me... and Jack?' There was incredulity but also a hint of fear in her voice.

'I'm afraid so, and the sooner he's arrested, the better. Would you mind if I make a call to the inspector from in here where there's less likelihood of us being overheard?' She nodded and I made the call.

I got straight through to Giulia Trevisan and she listened intently. 'You could well be right, Dan. It fits. Where is Baker now?'

'I'm not sure. I presume he's still on the island but I'll go and look for him now. Don't worry, I'll wait until you get here for the arrest, but I just want to be absolutely sure that he isn't planning to make another attempt on Alice's life.'

'Give me fifteen minutes and I'll be there.' There was a pause. 'Be careful, Dan. If he is our man, remember he's already killed twice.'

25

SUNDAY AFTERNOON

Leaving Alice in the cool of her office, I took Oscar for a walk around the gardens. A glance at the swimming pool revealed Desmond Norman once again swimming gently up and down while Rocco Gentile did press-ups on the tiles at the far end, under the appreciative eyes of Maggie McBride on a sunbed. A bit further over, Diego was working in the shade, transplanting some flowers from one bed to another, and he gave me an enquiring look as I passed, but I didn't have time to stop for now. I called in at my room to check the accommodation list and saw that Freddie Baker and Antoinette Latour had been allocated room five. I walked past it but was unable to tell without knocking whether there was anybody in there. However, half of the equation was answered almost immediately, when I spotted Antoinette lying on a sunbed in the shade of one of the umbrella pines. I went over to her, doing my best to look and sound casual.

'Definitely far too hot to be out in the direct sunshine.'

She glanced up at me and smiled while Oscar trotted over for a cuddle, but I could see that she was struggling. Again, trying to look blasé, I pretended to scan my surroundings. 'No Freddie? Is he not a fan of the sun?'

Her expression became more serious. 'He's taken some stuff down to the boat. I think he's keen to make a quick getaway as soon as the inspector says so.' She hesitated. 'Or maybe he just wants to get away from me. We've just had a major argument, and I've told him it's all over between us.'

Although I was curious to know why they had been arguing, I had no time to stop and talk. Freddie Baker was my number-one priority for now.

I thanked her and hurried off in the direction of the main entrance to check that Freddie Baker wasn't thinking of leaving – but I was too late. I was just going through the archway and onto the downward ramp when I heard a throaty roar from ahead of me. I took the ramp at a gallop and when I emerged into the sunlight on the jetty, I was just in time to see Freddie Baker in his slick-looking speedboat, pulling away from the island. Clearly, he had either got fed up and was leaving to distance himself from Antoinette after she had had the temerity to dump him, or he'd somehow worked out that we were onto him and was trying to make his getaway. I turned and ran back up the ramp and into the garden to call Diego. My shout echoed around the garden and I saw a few heads look up, including Diego's. My tone must have got to him because he came running.

'Yes, Dan, what is it? Is something wrong?'

'It's Freddie Baker. He's just gone off in his speedboat and we need to stop him.'

He didn't need to be asked twice. Together, we ran back down to the jetty and he leapt into the launch with Oscar while I undid the mooring ropes. The engine sprang into life and I jumped aboard as he pulled away. As soon as we were moving, I pulled out my phone and called the inspector.

'Baker has just left in his speedboat. It looks as though he's heading back to Venice itself, maybe towards the Grand Canal.'

'Right, I'll put out an APB. I'm just setting off now. Do you think he's suspicious? Has he been spooked?'

'I don't think so. It's not like he's travelling fast. I certainly haven't said anything to him, but his girlfriend indicated that they've just had a big bust-up and he'd taken a bag down to the boat. According to what he told her, he just wanted to be ready to leave in a hurry when you say the word, but now I reckon he's trying to get away from his girlfriend, or maybe from the crime scene. Whether this is because he's got a guilty conscience, or because he's just fed up, is something we'll find out. I'm in the launch with Diego, and we're about a couple of hundred metres behind him, both boats observing the speed limit. We'll keep him in sight but we'll leave confronting him to you.'

We followed Freddie Baker for five minutes or so in the direction of San Marco. All was going smoothly as we approached the Doge's Palace and the line of hotels and restaurants on the quay before it, with both boats still more or less obeying the lagoon speed limit, when I distinctly saw Baker turn his head and look back in our direction. He must have registered that he was being followed because only a handful of seconds later, there was a powerful roar and the bow of the speedboat rose up in the water as he opened the throttle.

Diego reacted immediately and I was almost thrown backwards as he, too, accelerated hard. Alice's beautiful, polished launch clearly had a powerful engine as well, and he managed more or less to keep pace with the speedboat as it flew across the water towards the entrance to the Grand Canal. Baker kept casting anxious looks back towards us, but when two police launches appeared coming down the Grand Canal towards him, blue lights flashing, he must have panicked. He suddenly spun the wheel and headed sharply to the right, into a much narrower side canal.

Diego glanced across at me and shouted, 'He's crazy going down there at that speed. I'll do my best to follow him, but you'd better hang on tight.'

With this, he threw the launch into a turn so sharp, we were almost perpendicular to the water for a while and followed the wake of the speedboat. Seconds later, we were flying up a frighteningly narrow canal in Baker's wake, waves breaking against the five- or six-hundred-year-old buildings on either side, and the spray soaking us. Diego was concentrating hard, while I gritted my teeth and hung onto the side of the boat with one hand, my other arm wrapped around Oscar to stop him being thrown out – although he looked as if he was enjoying himself immensely. Glancing over my shoulder, I saw one of the blue and white police launches tearing up the canal behind us. I was vaguely aware of the disapproving looks of bystanders, and the frightened screams of tourists on the low humpbacked bridges as Freddie's speedboat bumped its way under them with a tortured scraping noise. Diego showed his professionalism by managing to follow at pace, but without our launch so much as grazing the sides.

A moment or two later, Diego pointed straight ahead of us. In the distance, a rubbish barge was completely blocking the way. He turned towards me and shouted, 'All he can do now is take a left just before the barge. He'll then be forced to go left again and head back in the opposite direction. That canal runs parallel to this one, less than a hundred metres away. Do you feel like jumping out and running across? Maybe you can catch him if he decides to get out and make a run for it.' Even before I started to formulate an answer, he had thrown the engines into reverse and the water boiled and hissed around us as we slowed almost to a halt. He manoeuvred the boat expertly against the side of the canal and I managed to scramble out. My intention was to leave Oscar with him, but Oscar had other ideas. As I started running down a narrow alley, barely wider than my shoulders, in the direction of Diego's pointing finger, I almost tripped over as Oscar came shooting past me, tail wagging wildly, having a wonderful time.

We emerged from the alley onto a paved path beside the other canal, with a line of blue and red working boats moored along the far side of it. The roar of the approaching speedboat echoed around the houses, although I couldn't yet see it. I searched in vain for something I could push or drop into the canal so as to slow the speedboat before deciding that, if all else failed, I would have to do it myself. I ran along to the next bridge, pushing a group of tourists out of the way as I readied myself on the parapet. I was vaguely aware of Oscar's front paws appearing alongside my hands as we both stared over the low wall, but my attention was riveted on the point about fifty yards away where the side canal emerged into this one. As I looked on, the speed-boat screamed around the ninety-degree bend, hopelessly out of control. It bounced heavily against a moored boat on the other side before zigzagging towards me with Freddie Baker clearly visible, desperately spinning the wheel.

The good news from my point of view was that these manoeuvres had reduced his speed considerably, and when the boat reached the bridge on which I was standing, I took a deep breath and leapt.

What happened next wasn't my finest hour. I landed awkwardly, with one foot on the seat alongside the driver and the other on the slippery deck, causing me to fall sideways and bang my shoulder against the side of the boat. A fraction of a second later, there was a thud as fifty pounds of canine bone and muscle hit me in what's politely referred to as the lower abdomen, and I doubled up in pain, totally winded. The boat ricocheted under the bridge like a ball in a pinball machine and continued down the canal, bouncing off the moored boats and the stone walls. Still clutching myself in agony, I opened my eyes to see Freddie Baker above me, reaching for what looked like a starting handle, certainly something big, metallic and heavy. He came towards me and raised it above his head. I tried to get up, but my feet slipped on the wet deck, and I held up an arm in a probably vain attempt to protect myself from the impending blow.

But the blow didn't come.

There was a squeal and I opened my eyes again to see Freddie Baker with Oscar's teeth sunk into one of his flashy gold trainers, doing his best to tug him off balance. I was still registering the fact that this was one of the very few times I'd ever seen Oscar attempt to bite anybody, when the boat slewed under yet another low bridge. This time, the clearance between the top of the boat and the bridge was almost non-existent and a second later, there was a heavy thump as the stonework caught Freddie Baker across the shoulders and the back of the head, throwing him onto the deck behind me, where he landed in an unconscious heap. Out of control, but with its speed now considerably reduced, the speedboat veered sharply and nosedived into the wall of the canal, wedging itself between two moored boats and coming to a halt. Mercifully, this also had the effect of stopping the engine, and the ensuing silence was almost deafening.

As I lay there, sucking in huge gulps of air and clutching myself, trying to work out if my shoulder or my nether regions were the more painful, something surreal happened. I looked up from the deck of the boat to a little balcony with wrought-iron railings protruding at first-floor level from one of the houses lining the canal. Up there, I could see the figure of a man, considerably older than me, with a mop of long, white hair hanging down to his shoulders. He could have been a medieval depiction of God. He looked down at me with a benevolent expression and, to my surprise, produced what looked like a mandolin from his side and began to play. I've no idea what the tune was, but the slow, melancholy rhythm had a calming effect on me.

But not on Oscar.

Certain sounds have the effect of encouraging Oscar to start singing and, as I lay there, my Labrador launched into a canine accompaniment to the music that echoed up and down the canal. Tuneful, it wasn't, but I didn't have the breath to tell him to shut up and let the man play.

It came as a considerable relief less than a minute later when two blue and white police launches arrived from different directions, with Diego just behind one of them. They slowed to a halt alongside the battered remains of the speedboat, and I saw that one of them contained some familiar faces, among them Giulia Trevisan. Her arrival did the trick. Oscar stopped howling and started wagging his tail as he recognised who had come to see him.

'Are you all right, Dan?' Giulia sounded concerned, and I attempted a reassuring wave as Constable Piave jumped athletically onto the rear of the speedboat and crouched down alongside the supine figure of Freddie Baker. He was followed by Sergeant Scarpa, who came over to see how I was. With his assistance, I managed to straighten up and he helped me onto one of the luxurious seats. I gave him a grateful look.

'Thanks a lot. I wouldn't recommend jumping off the bridges.'

'I'll bear that in mind, *Commissario*.' He smiled and glanced back to where the constable was still crouching beside Freddie Baker. 'How's he doing, Piave?'

'It looks like he's just coming round now. No blood, but he's going to have a headache tomorrow.'

Above us, the godlike musician came to the end of his performance and sat back to a ripple of applause. A crowd was gathering on both sides of the canal around us and this, as much as anything else, finally spurred me into action. I leant forward and stroked Oscar's ears. 'Thanks, old buddy, that's another one I owe you.'

Oscar looked up and gave me a toothy grin. At this rate, he was going to be eating steak for weeks to come.

26

SUNDAY AFTERNOON

Somewhat gingerly, I climbed back into Alice's launch with Oscar. After helping me on board, Diego confessed that the chase through the canals had fulfilled a long-held ambition of his.

'I've spent all of my life chugging around here at little more than walking pace. I know it's bad for the foundations of the buildings, but being able to tear up the rule book just once has been immensely satisfying.'

He was most appreciative both of my acrobatics – however poorly executed – and of the performance of the musician on the balcony. He told me that the instrument the man had been playing was an old favourite, a lute, and the tune a traditional Venetian seafaring song about a sailor who returns to his loved one after months on the ocean wave. It occurred to me that I would also be quite happy to return to my own loved one in Florence after what had been an eventful weekend.

The trip back to the island was conducted at far slower speed, and I was more than happy to sit back, nursing my shoulder, and enjoy the sights. When we emerged from the network of narrow canals, we passed beneath the Bridge of Sighs, and Diego told me this had gained the name as it connected the Doge's Palace and court of law with the ancient prison. Hopefully, Freddie Baker would also now face a long spell in prison for the two brutal murders he had committed – all for the sake of money. This reminded me to pull out my phone and call my dad to thank him for his advice and to tell him that we had cracked the case. He sounded happy for me and maybe a bit envious. As I gradually massage my bruised shoulder, I reflected that jumping off a bridge onto a moving boat was one experience I wouldn't be in a hurry to repeat.

Sergeant Scarpa followed us back to the island in a police launch and informed everybody that they could now leave. I stood alongside him and translated as he broke the news that Freddie Baker was a murderer who had struck twice. Antoinette looked appalled, but not too saddened, and the reaction of most of the others was one of relief and satisfaction. To my surprise, I received an unexpectedly hearty handshake from Desmond Norman and kisses from Maggie McBride and even Sandra Groves. I wondered if Alice had had a chance to sit down with each of them and talk about their part in her autobiography, but I didn't make any mention of that to them.

It occurred to me that since my arrival here on the island on Friday, nobody had mentioned my books, and my hopes of a Hollywood film deal had melted away. To my surprise, I almost felt relieved. After what I'd learned about Hollywood in the last forty-eight hours, I wasn't too sure how badly I wanted to be involved with that kind of thing. Maybe writing a few paperbacks and a job as a private investigator was going to be a far more satisfying way of life.

Alice also looked relieved. After hearing of Diego's prowess at the wheel of the launch, and of what she called my heroic exploits – and personally inspecting my bruised shoulder – she insisted that I stay until next morning. She was looking far more cheerful than before, and although I was sure that this was in no small part due to the fact that we'd managed to catch the killer in our midst, it was also patently because things were going well between her and Mary. I spotted Mary briefly as I walked back to my room and she gave me a sparkling smile, which appeared to indicate that she, too, was very happy with the way things had worked out. I rejoiced for them.

When I got back to my room, I took a couple of paracetamol and lay down for a rest. I must have gone out like a light, and it was almost six by the time I opened my eyes and headed for the shower while Oscar continued to snore happily on the blanket beside the bed. My bruised shoulder was now a Technicolor shade of purple, but the warm water of the shower and the painkillers I'd taken meant that I could move it normally. I dressed and we went outside into the fresh air.

Valentina and her daughter were already busy stripping the beds in the now empty guest rooms and both gave me a cheery greeting. They asked how I was feeling, and I was quick to reassure them that I was doing fine. Valentina even stopped work for a few moments to query what her husband had no doubt already told her.

'Is it true that you really jumped off a bridge into a speedboat?'

'It was a very low bridge and a slow speedboat. If I'd timed it a bit better, I wouldn't even have fallen over.'

'And the man with the silly shoes, why did he kill these people?'

'Money, mainly. I think he was an unhappy character and his frustration just boiled over.'

'And Diego said he tried to kill you with a huge great wrench.'

'He certainly tried but, luckily, my four-legged friend came to my rescue. I don't suppose you've got an odd bit of steak for him, have you?'

Valentina nodded and assured me that she would see that Oscar was suitably rewarded. 'Miss Graceland's having another party tonight – not a big one, just for us – and Diego's going to barbecue some meat. She told me when I saw you to ask you to go over to see her. She wants to talk to you.'

Alice was sitting under the pergola with Mary at her side. There was a champagne bottle in an ice bucket and glasses on the table in front of them. Alice waved me over and got up to kiss me on both cheeks before crouching down to make a fuss of Oscar. 'Thank you so much for everything you've done this week-end, Dan. I hope your poor injured shoulder doesn't hurt too much.'

'I'm fine, thanks. To be honest, looking back on what happened, considering that there were a couple of police launches involved in the chase, it was probably a pretty stupid and unnecessary thing to do, but at moments like that, you don't really have time to stop and think.'

'Well, the important thing is that you're fine. And now, my daughter and I would be very pleased if you would be so good as to open this bottle of champagne, and we can have a toast.' Her expression of satisfaction when she spoke of her daughter was a joy to see.

I reached for the bottle and shot a smile across towards Mary as I did so. 'Have you got over the shock yet? It's been quite a weekend, hasn't it? Two murders and then this amazing news. You could be excused for feeling a bit overwhelmed.'

Mary stood up and came over to my side to help with the glasses. Close up, I could see that her eyes were still red. I could well imagine the emotions that must have been coursing through her body all day.

'Yes, it's taken me a long time, but I'm beginning to come to terms with everything.' Her voice became more husky. 'I thought my mum had died a few months ago and now I find that I've got another one. I've been on an emotional roller coaster, but I'm getting there.' She shot an affectionate glance across at Alice. 'It's probably going to take a while before I get the hang of calling you Mum, but I'll manage.'

We all sat down and Alice held up her glass to clink it against ours. 'I couldn't be happier. Neither of you can possibly imagine what the last twenty-five years of my life have been like. Not a single day has passed without me thinking of the little baby I had to give up.' She looked across at Mary with an expression of desperation in her eyes. 'I know it was the selfish way out, but I was under contract to one of the biggest studios at that time, and if word had got out that I'd had an illegitimate child, they would have sacked me on the spot, and my career would have been finished. I don't expect you to forgive me, Mary, but all I can tell you is that I've regretted it every day of my life, and maybe you will at least pity me. Seeing you now, grown into a beautiful, intelligent and successful woman, has been the greatest satisfaction of my life. Forget the Oscars and the Emmys; this is what true happiness is all about.' She held the glass aloft 'To Mary.'

I joined in the toast and took a sip of the predictably excellent champagne. I was dying to ask why Alice had chosen to reveal everything to Mary on this day of all days, but I felt that this was a personal question and best avoided. I was therefore very interested in the course of the conversation when Alice volunteered the information, addressing herself to me, almost as if in a confessional.

'Although Mary never knew it, I followed her life and her career from afar. On countless occasions, I've had to fight hard to resist the temptation to go and see her and tell her everything, but it wouldn't have been fair. She was fortunate to have a wonderful, caring family who loved her every bit as much as I could have done and, however much I might have missed her, I knew I couldn't break up a family.' Tears appeared in her eyes once again and, alongside her, I could see Mary reaching for her tissue as well.

Predictably, Oscar stood up on his hind legs and stretched up to nuzzle Alice's chin before turning to Mary and repeating the process. As for me, I stayed quiet and waited for Alice to pick up her story again.

'Two things happened this Easter. Rose, my long-time PA, finally married her man and moved to Australia with him, and the news broke that Mary's adoptive mother had passed away. I could imagine how distressed Mary would be and I had to suppress the instinct to run to her to explain everything and offer comfort. Instead, I knew she needed time to grieve and I also knew that I couldn't just spring my news on her without giving her the chance to get to know me first. That's why I managed to engineer a drinks reception for media journalists and academics where I would have the opportunity of meeting and speaking to Mary's tutor. She put me in touch with Mary and, as a result, I managed to persuade her to come over here to work for me but, really, so she could get to know me.'

I was fascinated and could well imagine what must be going through the heads of both women. Seeing as the conversation had already taken a very personal turn, I felt I could ask the other question that had been intriguing me.

'And what about Mary's father? How are things there?'

I was pleasantly surprised to hear Mary answer the question. 'Really well. You can probably imagine how stunned I've been to realise that my true parents are two of the best-known faces in the world. That, also, is going to take me some time to digest, but he's been super – considering that it all must have come as such a shock to him as well. He had to go back to the US this evening because he's working on a movie over there, but I'm going to meet up with him again in a few weeks' time.'

Alice added a few words. 'My plan was to get Dirk here and only then to sit down with Mary and tell her the truth. I thought I owed it to her to give her the opportunity to meet both of her real parents at the same time.' She wiped her eyes and even managed to produce a hint of a smile. 'I must confess that I was a bit apprehensive – make that scared stiff – about how Dirk was going to receive the news, but I couldn't have hoped for better. Maybe he's not such a bad guy after all.'

Something else occurred to me. 'Talking of bad guys, did you manage to sit down and speak to the people you mentioned in your autobiography? How did they react?'

The little smile returned to Alice's face. 'A few surprises. Desmond Norman apologised profusely, and I genuinely got the impression he meant what he said. Under pressure from Greg, Carlos finally told me what happened that night up on top of the tower at his house. That was before he'd come out as gay, and he'd been up there with his boyfriend of the time. They argued and his boyfriend turned away in a huff, tripped over something, slipped, and fell to his death. Carlos tried to catch him as he fell, but without success. The reason he didn't tell this to the police was depressingly similar to my own experience. He knew this would have meant revealing his sexuality, probably seriously damaging his career. Hollywood wasn't anything like as liberated then as it is now.'

'So does this mean you're going to leave Norman and Rodriguez out of your book?'

Alice nodded. 'They both get a mention, but nothing negative. Alastair Groves and his devil wife are staying in. Would you believe they both refused even to speak to me before they left? I owe it to Lucy to hang them out to dry. If it hadn't been for Alastair, Lucy would probably still be alive today and a bigger star than I ever was.'

'And Maggie McBride?'

'There's no way she'll ever change. She is what she is but, deep down, she's not bad with it. She had the decency to apologise for her affair with Dirk and, in return, I've wiped her slate clean. She'll still get quite a few mentions in the book, but I'll tone down the language.'

'And the comment on her card last night about her poisoning her husband. Was that based on fact, or just for the sake of the murder mystery?'

Alice shook her head. 'I made that up. She may be many things, but she isn't a killer.' Her smile broadened. 'You might be interested to know that you're going to get a mention as well – and Oscar, of course.'

I smiled back. 'Oscar and I thank you. I look forward to reading it at leisure when it comes out.'

As the sun began to set behind us, we carried on talking – or, rather, Alice and her daughter did a lot of talking while I sat quietly, reflecting on the events of the last forty-eight hours. Behind us, Diego and Guido fired up the barbecue while Gabriella prepared a table for seven people. I was touched to see that Alice was including Valentina's family and me in tonight's celebration dinner.

At just before seven, my phone started ringing. It was Giulia Trevisan and she had news.

'*Ciao*, Dan. Forensics have just finished searching Baker's speedboat, and guess what they've just found in there? A little plastic bag scrunched up in a waste bin with some specks of grey powder still caught in the corners. No prizes for guessing what that is. He can cry to his lawyer as much as he likes, but we've nailed him, and I'm just calling to say a huge thank you to you for everything you've done, and for making sure he didn't escape. I couldn't have done it without you.'

'That's very nice of you to say so, but you would have got him without me, I'm quite sure. Remember to give Virgilio and me a shout if you're ever in Tuscany, and we'll see that you get a good meal.'

A few minutes later, Valentina arrived to call us to table. This was laden with different salads, dishes of roast vegetables, and a silver salver in the middle piled high with everything from spare ribs and grilled chicken to lamb chops and fillet steak, but, fortunately, no cauliflower. Before Diego started serving, he looked across the table and caught my eye.

'Here, Dan, you asked me to do something special for Oscar. Miss Graceland thought this might be suitable.' He handed me over a plate on which there was a huge chunk of fillet steak. As I placed it down on the floor at my feet, his eyes opened wide with anticipation and he glanced up at me for a moment.

I gave him a grin. 'All yours, Oscar. You earned it.'

I swear he winked at me before burying his nose in the reward he so richly deserved.

He really is a very good dog.

* * *

MORE FROM T. A. WILLIAMS

Another book from T. A. Williams, is available to order now here: https://mybook.to/DuomoOscarBackAd

ACKNOWLEDGEMENTS

Warmest thanks to Emily Ruston, my lovely editor at the marvellous Boldwood Books, as well as the rest of the Boldwood team. Sincere thanks also to Sue Smith and Emily Reader for picking up all my errors and making sure that everything makes sense. Special thanks to the talented Simon Mattacks for narrating the audio versions of all the books in the Dan and Oscar series. To me, he sounds just like Dan should sound. Finally, thanks to Mariangela, my wife, for all her help, advice and support.

ABOUT THE AUTHOR

T. A. Williams is the author of The Armstrong and Oscar Cozy Mystery Series, cosy crime stories set in his beloved Italy, featuring the adventures of DCI Armstrong and his labrador Oscar. Trevor lives in Devon with his Italian wife.

Download your exclusive bonus content from T. A. Williams here:

Visit T. A. Williams' website: www.tawilliamsbooks.com

Follow T. A. Williams' on social media:

 facebook.com/TrevorWilliamsBooks

 x.com/TAWilliamsBooks

 bsky.app/profile/tawilliamsbooks.bsky.social

ALSO BY T. A. WILLIAMS

The Armstrong and Oscar Cozy Mystery Series

Murder in Tuscany

Murder in Chianti

Murder in Florence

Murder in Siena

Murder at the Matterhorn

Murder at the Leaning Tower

Murder on the Italian Riviera

Murder in Portofino

Murder in Verona

Murder in the Tuscan Hills

Murder at the Ponte Vecchio

Murder on an Italian Island

Murder in Venice

Standalone Novels

Under a Spanish Sky

Boldwood

Boldwood Books is an award-winning fiction publishing company seeking out the best stories from around the world.

Find out more at www.boldwoodbooks.com

Join our reader community for brilliant books, competitions and offers!

Follow us
@BoldwoodBooks
@TheBoldBookClub

Sign up to our weekly deals newsletter

https://bit.ly/BoldwoodBNewsletter

Printed in Dunstable, United Kingdom